CAVEAT

ALSO BY LAURA KALPAKIAN

Graced Land

These Latter Days
(now a John F. Blair trade paperback)

Crescendo

Dark Continent and Other Stories

Fair Augusto and Other Stories

Cosette: The Sequel to Les Misérables

Beggars and Choosers

CAVEAT

LAURA KALPAKIAN

JOHN F. BLAIR, PUBLISHER
WINSTON-SALEM, NORTH CAROLINA

Copyright © 1998 by Laura Kalpakian
All rights reserved
Printed in the United States of America

Front jacket photo: Coalinga. National Oil Co. Tanks and Refining (circa 1914)
from the *Coalinga, California, Photograph Album,*
BANC PIC 1984.073—ALB,
The Bancroft Library, University of California, Berkeley.
Originally in black-and-white, this photo has been specially tinted
and cropped.

Design: Liza Langrall

*All of the characters in this novel are fictitious, and any resemblance to
actual persons, living or dead, is purely coincidental.*

Library of Congress Cataloging-in-Publication Data

Kalpakian, Laura.
    Caveat / Laura Kalpakian.
      p.   cm.
    ISBN 0-89587-223-4 (alk. paper)
    I. Title.
PS3561.A4168C38   1998
813'.54—dc21   98-14592

This book is for Sandra Thomas.

ACKNOWLEDGMENTS

The author wishes to thank Carolyn Sakowski, Steve Kirk, and the staff at John F. Blair, Publisher. Thanks too are due to Deborah Schneider, Juliet Burton, Cindy Hazen, and Mike Freeman. Closer to home: over the years, Bear and Brendan lived bravely with this novel; Peggy K. Johnson typed it many times; Meredith Cary read it many times; and William J. Johnson painted around it more than once.

Rain set in about dark. . . . I made a sort of pillow of my gun, cartridge box, haversack and canteen and stretched myself out on the brush pile, tired to death. [The Union army replacement troops began] forming a line in the darkness. Their regimental bands played continuously and it seemed to me that they all played the tune of "The Girl I Left Behind Me." And the rain drizzled down, while every fifteen minutes from the river one of the big guns roared and sent a ponderous shell shrieking into the ravine in the direction of the enemy. To this day, whenever I hear an instrumental band playing "The Girl I Left Behind Me," there comes to me the memory of that gloomy Sunday night at Shiloh. I hear again the ceaseless patter of the rain, the dull heavy tread of the marching columns, the thunderous roar of the navy guns, the demoniacal scream of the projectile and mingled with it all is the sweet plaintive music of that old song.

Leander Stillwell
Private, Sixty-first Indiana Infantry, Union army
Writing in 1916 about the Battle of Shiloh in
The Story of a Common Soldier

Time will rust the sharpest sword,
Time will consume the strongest cord;
That which molders hemp and steel,
Mortal arm and nerve must feel.

Sir Walter Scott
1817

NOVEMBER

1916

CHAPTER ONE

The St. Elmo train station, a huge, clay-colored Moorish monstrosity, had four squat towers, and each wore a toupee of ivy, all askew. The windows were fancifully grilled with wrought-iron lyres, suggesting a theatrical past, and out front, iron spears resting on ornate posts served to tether horses. Four men, clearly official, corpulent and soberly clad, alighted from a gleaming Locomobile and hastened along the station arcades. Their footsteps grated audibly, even within the cool vaulted waiting room. Noting that the westbound from Arizona had not yet arrived, they hurried through the station to the crowded platform, where a slightly fetid breeze from the nearby stockyards disturbed the hovering flies. The four men restlessly checked their gold pocket watches, nodding agreeably to their fellow citizens who were meeting this same train for other, less pressing reasons.

They were sleek men, girded with flesh, years, and contentment. Their hands were white and soft as bread dough, their hair clipped, shoes shined. The four represented the civic union of commerce and politics, each routinely elected to one public office or another while they plunged their hands into private tills as well. Sid Ferris, owner of the New Town Hotel and other properties, was currently mayor. Art Whickham represented the city's oldest bank and one of its oldest families. Otis McGahey, a lawyer, represented Art's bank and Sid's hotel and his own interests. Judge Lew Cannon represented the judiciary, if not justice. But at this moment, they all wore the same expression of collective anxiety.

"I still say it's risky," said Sid Ferris, tucking his watch back in his waistcoat.

"Everything's risky," Art Whickham replied gruffly. Art was the shortest of the quartet, trim, dapper, mustachioed, and bristling.

"We all but promised the voters rain. I just hope Hank Beecham can deliver."

"Look what he did up north last year," remarked Otis McGahey. Otis had a lawyer's love of precedent. "They brought in Hank Beecham and he brought in five inches of rain. Saved the whole town. Saved their crops. You read the testimonials. They was dying like flies in Santa Rosita."

"Where are all these flies coming from anyway?" asked Art, batting at them with his hat.

Otis nodded in the direction of the stockyards. "Cattle can't stand it. They drop where they stand. Three hundred and one straight days without rain."

"Three hundred and two," Judge Lew Cannon corrected him. "It's God's curse on us. God's cursed St. Elmo with drought before. We ought to wait for God. He delivered us in 1911." Lew Cannon wore a gray patriarch's beard and had the heavy-lidded, thick-limbed bearing of a deliberate man. He spoke slowly and with practiced Almighty inflections.

"Yes," said Sid Ferris, a shudder rattling his fleshy uphol-stered frame. "He delivered and He ruined. That flood swept my whole hotel away."

"Near swept everything away," McGahey observed. A pale man with red hair receding rapidly over his freckled pate, Otis wheezed and flushed under duress.

"We been over this before," Art reminded them curtly, just as he and the others were required to execute short re-spectful bows to a delegation from the Ladies' Culture League, a group of matrons—including their own wives—who moved in a silken mass, rather like a herd of jellyfish.

"Yes," added Lew Cannon in a dour voice after the ladies had passed, "but that flood was only a few years ago and we ought to remember the damage done then."

Art turned to him savagely. "You want to remind the voters, Lew?"

Judge Cannon sulked. "I still say we're interfering with God's plan if we hire someone to reverse His will."

"Save it for Sunday," Art snapped.

Like the others, Art was a devout church member. St. Elmo, California, boasted a Baptist chapel and the African Redeemed Church of the Lamb, which didn't actually have a church, but its believers gathered under the Reverend Eli Washington's spellbinding voice every Sunday in a warehouse, and their music and hosannas echoed in the empty streets. The Catholic Church of the Assumption served the needs of the Mexican and Irish populations. At one time, there had been a Chinese temple, but it had burned in 1909, and now the Chinese implored their gods privately. Despite this display of religious tolerance and plurality, the city's elite remained—as it had always been—solidly Methodist and Mormon. Of these four, Sid was Methodist; Art and Lew and Otis were Mormons.

The men busied themselves looking downright Augustan, greeting voters till the train came in at last, billowing smoke and steam, splashing cinders and ash, screeching like a beast brought down in defeat. People on the platform pressed forward as the doors opened, and passengers disembarked amid a bevy of greetings and reunions. The four men watched expectantly as the westbound disgorged dusty women with drooping feathers on their hats, fussy children, bland-faced workingmen, natty commercial travelers, and even an opera impresario from Chicago, who was met by the ladies from the Culture League. The four men again doffed their hats as the ladies passed by with their impresario in tow. The impresario wore a carnation in his buttonhole; a garland of gleaming mustache luxuriated across his face, and he had a dark complexion and long-lashed, liquid brown eyes.

"He looks like a Mex to me," said Art under his breath.

"Signor Federicci," said Otis. "My wife says he's Italian."

Art's features did a swift dance of derision around his nose, and he muttered a few choice observations on Signor Federicci's ancestral origins.

As the platform throng thinned and their rainmaker did not appear, Sid Ferris asked if anyone could remember what Hank Beecham looked like. No one could till Lew Cannon, older than the others, remarked succinctly, "Like his old man." He nodded as the last passenger stepped down. "Remember?"

Having pinned their hopes on Hank Beecham, the four were disappointed. He had none of the jaunty confidence expected of a miracle worker. His lanky body appeared pinned together hastily, and his limbs refused to work in unison. Collarless, carrying his coat and hat and a single battered satchel, he wore crumpled pants and shirt, the seams frayed, his clothes pocked with cinder holes, his boots gray with dust. His hair was sparse, lusterless, and long, his face weathered as the west wall of a desert barn. He walked right up to them.

"Well, if it ain't Hank Beecham!" Sid Ferris, with a hotel owner's bonhomie, clapped him on the back. A puff of dust or powder wafted from the rainmaker's clothes. "Hank Beecham, our native son. What's it been? Twenty years? More? I'd know you anywhere, Hank. Welcome home!"

Without smiling, Hank Beecham shook hands with the four, who were reluctant to put their white hands into his. Beecham's hands were quilted with scars, hairless, and hard. His eyes were pale, vacant, and blue and the eyelashes, eyebrows, and mustache singed so many times they appeared to be mere sketches upon his face, as though the Creator had planned to include them but forgot the final execution. From his body came the faint unmistakable odor of gunpowder. "You need rain, all right." That was the first thing Hank Beecham said, as he rolled himself a cigarette and lit it, striking the wooden lucifer on the buckle of his suspenders.

The four steered him through the station and out to Art's Locomobile. A horse tied nearby whinnied in protest at their approach and unceremoniously relieved itself all too near Art's shoes, obliging him to dance an unexpected jig as he opened the door. "We've made arrangements for you at the New Town Hotel. You're Sid's guest."

"Don't even think of paying, Hank," said Sid, taking the satchel, which was unexpectedly heavy.

"New Town?"

"Didn't you hear? We had quite the flood in 1911, and it wiped out most of the old town—of what you'd remember, anyway. Even wiped out Sid's old hotel," Otis informed him. Otis was a puffy man who perspired easily.

"But I rebuilt in New Town," Sid added proudly. "Bigger and better than ever. Electric light. Two baths on every floor. Why, this whole town is different! Improved! We built up from the ashes."

"I thought you said it was a flood," Hank remarked drily.

"God's cursed us again with drought," Lew Cannon began.

"Just step right in here," said Art, interrupting the judge. Hank took the front seat. The other three men were obliged to squeeze all too intimately in the backseat. "Yes, Hank, we're taking you to the New Town Hotel. We didn't think you'd want to stay all the way out at your family's old place. Your brother Horace and his boy, Earl, haven't had much luck there."

"Nobody had much luck there," said Hank.

Nobody contested this. Indeed, as president of the St. Elmo National Bank and Trust, Art Whickham had been prevailed upon by the other three not to foreclose on Hank's brother and nephew—at least not until St. Elmo had its rain.

Art had reminded them that Hank Beecham hadn't seen or spoken to his brother in more than twenty years. "I don't care," Sid Ferris had replied. "Blood is thicker than water. Blood is thicker than rain." To this, Art had merely observed that no Beecham's blood was any thicker than cheap whiskey, but he held off foreclosing just the same.

Of all the Beechams, Hank was the only one graced with so much as a morsel of luck. His father's luck had begun and ended with the Civil War, which is to say he lived through it. Jeremiah Beecham had fought with the Confederacy, the Third Army Corps, forty thousand strong, at Shiloh, one of the Yell Rifles under Brigadier General Patrick Cleburne of Arkansas. General Cleburne's troops led the Confederate attack at Shiloh that bloody Sunday morning in April 1862, surprising the Union army at breakfast. Beecham fought in the thick of it, the Hornet's Nest, the peach orchard, the fighting so terrible that when it was over, corpses covered the ground for acres. Though Cleburne's men were decimated—a third of their number dead, dying, wounded—Jeremiah Beecham lived to fight again the second day of Shiloh, when the Confederates were defeated. At Shiloh, he took a bullet in the cheek that exited through his mouth, which was open at the time. He took a bullet in the thigh at Missionary Ridge in 1863. He carried a couple of spent cartridges in his body from other engagements and powder burns along his neck and hands all his life, but he survived.

His luck alone would have got him promoted, but he couldn't read or write, and he remained a private in Cleburne's division.

Jeremiah could get teary on the subject of the immortal General Cleburne, the fightin'est Irishman who ever drew breath and the bravest and smartest general in the whole Confederate States of America. *If Old Pat hadda been commander, he woulda saved the Confederacy, by God, and there'd be slavery right now in the South.* Moreover, Jeremiah would whup any scoundrel—*You jes' name yer weapons, name 'em! Fists, knives*—who suggested that Grant was a greater general than Cleburne. Jeremiah spit on Grant. Sherman too. They never should have won at Shiloh. Why, that first day—to hear Jeremiah tell it—Sherman's men were so surprised they were bayoneted sleeping in their tents. And Grant? Grant had his back to the Tennessee River that first night and nowhere to go. *Grant shoulda drowned in the Tennessee River. Woulda drowned too, 'cept for* . . .

For forty years, Jeremiah told these tales to men enthralled and men indifferent, to men who remembered the conflict and men born long after the War. His battle experience was vast, and his accounts were long, detailed, and grisly. Jeremiah maundered on drunkenly: lost opportunities, blunders, brutal weather, inaccurate intelligence, high-command bickering that condemned the Confederacy and Jeremiah Beecham to defeat.

But of all Jeremiah's battles, it was Shiloh—that bloody and contested piece of Tennessee ground—that he returned to again and again, as though perhaps in repetition lay understanding or redress. That first day of battle, Rebel commanders believed they had broken the Union army in the West. That Sunday night, Rebel commanders slept in Sherman's tent and Rebel troops looted the Union camps. But at the end of the second day, cruelly defeated, the Confederate army—including the ragged remnants of the Yell Rifles—retreated south. In the mud and rain, they straggled, stumbled, staggered, leaving Tennessee. From Shiloh, Jeremiah carried a queerly collapsed right cheek, the result of the bullet. From Shiloh, he took a sword, an Enfield rifle, a pair of epaulettes and brass buttons he'd cut from the uniform of a dead Union general.

Even the St. Elmo pawnbroker had granted these articles were genuine Union, if not genuine Union general, and they so often graced his shop that the sword had its own place of pride, hanging high above the counter. Eventually, these tokens were not redeemed, but they had been so often spoken of that the words themselves—*Enfield rifle, sword, epaulettes, buttons*—came to have solidity, girth, and weight of their own, came to have significance, to resonate with the honor of the Beechams.

In the ruinous aftermath of the War, Jeremiah Beecham had left the land of cotton and fetched up eventually in the

St. Elmo Valley, bringing with him his tired, sun-strained wife and three little sons. (A girl and Hank were born in California.) He homesteaded a hundred and sixty acres of land that would have daunted even a sober, hardworking, productive man, which Jeremiah was not. He had the mouth, the mind, eventually the palsied rattle of a man cursed with drink, and as the ranching went downhill, the curse accelerated, as though obeying the laws of physics. When the curse was on him, Jeremiah Beecham would have sold his own mother into slavery for a drink.

He was eloquent and brutal on the topic of slavery, and he regarded all black people as little better than runaway chattels without rights or honor. For their part, St. Elmo's black population avoided Beecham—drunk or sober—crossing any street he happened to be on. Jeremiah accepted this as a mark of respect, instead of seeing its implicit contempt. He could not have borne their contempt, especially since— he would wax on—it was galling and against the laws of nature to see a black man prospering when a white man could not, to see black families comfortable while white children had no shoes.

This anomaly was all the more bitter given the Beechams' glorious past. Given drink and a listener, indeed, given just drink, Jeremiah would augment his vivid accounts of Shiloh, Chickamauga, Missionary Ridge, all the rest of them—the smoke, the shot and shell, the bloody bayonets, the mud, the muskets, the buttons and sword, the epaulettes and Enfield rifle—with a sonorous lament for the things defeat had stolen from him: land, crops, slaves, an opulent home, prize stock, a stable of racehorses, a carriage (several carriages as the years passed), a pianny, and silver spoons. In truth, from the time Beechams had first crawled out of the alluvial Arkansas mud, they had clung by their fingernails to whatever scrap of land they'd tenanted, without even owning so much as a divot of sod. They could not even hope to inherit the earth, since they were not meek. If it wasn't for the dirty Yanks, Jeremiah would often hiccough in closing his soliloquy, he would yet be sitting on some well-swept veranda tended by dusky deferential servants.

It was in this vein—an ill-omened moment, a sentimental nod toward the Confederacy, the Lost Cause, the Bonnie Blue Flag, the Yell Rifles, and Patrick Cleburne—that Jeremiah Beecham named his St. Elmo ranch Shiloh. He was defeated there as surely as he had been at the original. His daughter ran off one night, taking with her the family's last horse and every cent Mrs. Eulalie Beecham had managed to scrape, hoard, and hide from her husband. Eulalie pleaded with Jeremiah that the daughter's defection meant one less mouth to feed. Enraged about the horse (he did not know about the money), Jeremiah went to the sheriff and drunkenly swore out a complaint for her arrest. The sheriff took it all down, although, alas, he could not act on it, as it had not been notarized. St. Elmo's civic servants never relax their sense of duty.

The eldest son inherited his father's taste for drink and died in a brawl before he was twenty. Another son was sent to prison for assault with a knife. He died there. Jeremiah himself, the old soldier, unaccountably lived on till 1906, succumbing finally to alcoholic convulsions. His third son, Horace, found him one day, dead, sprawled in the yard at Shiloh between the clapboard house and the splintering barn, the chickens cheerily picking him clean, louse by louse.

Horace, his frail wife, and his little son, Earl, saw Jeremiah decently into a grave (and one far distant from the grave of Mrs. Eulalie Beecham). And then Horace got drunk and tried to storm the pawnshop to redeem the sword, the Enfield, the epaulettes and brass buttons, his family's honor. Failing in this, he spent the night in jail and went home the next day.

Most of Shiloh had been sold off long before, the ranch reduced to a few acres, which Horace mortgaged to Art Whickham's bank. He drank for months on this money, happy as the proverbial pig in shit. Horace neither sowed nor reaped, but scraped by, enough to keep little Earl in shoes and make some of the mortgage payments. As the years passed, and certainly after his wife died, Horace gave up all pretense of ranching, and he and Earl, now a young man, kept no more livestock than the chickens, which, aside from the occasional coyote foray, required very little of them, scarcely even vigilance.

Hank Beecham did not drink. He may have looked like Jeremiah, but he was his mother's son. He had Eulalie Beecham's knack for study and invention, her sure steady hand, her long delicate fingers. His actual education was haphazard and incomplete—due mainly to a lack of shoes—but he put his time to good use. Before he was fifteen, he was doing a tidy business fixing things for people for miles around. His reputation spread, and sewing machines were his specialty. Hank Beecham could take a sewing machine that had been rusted shut since the Red Sea parted and make it hum again.

Before he was seventeen, Hank scraped together his fix-it earnings and left Shiloh for good. He took his mother with him. Without a tear or parting word, Eulalie left her husband and Horace to the bottle and the glories of the Confederacy. She and Henry moved into town, lived in two rooms above a little rented shop where Henry fixed things, his practice not limited to sewing machines. Eulalie kept the books for the shop and kept house for her son. Henry Beecham worked six days a week and on the seventh he rested not. He rested not ever.

Upon moving to town, he presented himself to the fledgling public library with inquiries after science and military history. The librarian showed him where he might best look, and he took his first two books, Thorpe's *Dictionary of Applied Chemistry* and Hardee's *Rifle and Light Infantry Tactics*, to a table near the works of Sir Walter Scott. On that shelf, he saw *Life of Napoleon Bonaparte* by Sir Walter, and he took that too.

Sitting across from him was Miss Emmons, teacher of the elementary grades at Pioneer School and a graduate of Spartana Normal School. Brown as a she-sparrow, Miss Emmons was tiny and birdlike, old enough to have a pinch to her lips and a bristle in her walk. She elicited from her students neither affection nor fear, nor anything really, save perhaps their easygoing contempt, so casual as to be scarcely deserving of the word. Winter and summer, Miss Emmons wore white, high-collared shirtwaists and black wool skirts, her clothes so oft-washed that the white darkened and the black faded, both to a dull off-brown matching the coat she donned for her daily walk from Sister Whitworth's board-inghouse to Pioneer School.

Miss Emmons was a regular patron of the struggling public library and took her work always to the table near Sir Walter Scott, out of loyalty to that prolific poet and author. Hank, on the other hand, was a creature of habit, and having once sat near Sir Walter, he returned as though obeying the dictates of cams and cranks on a sewing machine. For a while, Miss Emmons watched him struggle through his heavy tomes of science and history, using his index finger along the page and forming the words with difficulty on his lips. It was more than she could bear.

Eventually, Hank Beecham could be found several evenings a week in the empty classroom at Pioneer School, his ungainly frame tucked uncomfortably into a diminutive desk while Miss Emmons broadened his literacy skills and ciphering abilities. Once he caught on, Hank burned through books, though his interests were narrow, limited finally to military history and science, chemistry especially.

About this time, Hank Beecham began hiring a wagon on Saturday nights, though it was more visibly in use on Sunday mornings. When the godly gathered in churches and the godless tossed on crapulent beds, Hank drove his rented horse and wagon up into the foothills, occasionally accompanied by Miss Emmons. The sight of them together gave St. Elmo a communal guffaw, especially as Hank admitted he was conducting "chemical experiments." However, if the wind blew the right way, sometimes an acrid plume of smoke blew with it. A year or so later, the wagon was destroyed and the horse killed—blown to bits, actually—when it took a notion to run off and the chemicals and gunpowder in the wagon ignited in an unforeseen explosion. The godly came pouring from the churches and the godless came stumbling from their inebriate beds to look eastward. Hank was some distance from the blast. Miss Emmons was not with him.

Following this incident, the city council quickly added a

statute to the books prohibiting chemical experiments without a permit, which they were not about to grant. Hank didn't care. Eulalie Beecham was dying of a long terrible illness, and for the final months of her life, Hank gave up everything to care for her till she died. She was buried in the city cemetery. For the words of farewell, Hank prevailed on a good-natured Baptist (and made a donation), though no Beecham had ever set foot in his church. At the funeral, Hank nodded to the doctor who had attended Eulalie's last illness, but he was otherwise silent, not so much as a nod or word to Jeremiah or Horace, both of whom were sloshed. These four were the only mourners.

From the cemetery, Hank went directly to the repair shop and picked up the bag he had already packed. Thence to the printer, where he collected cards he had ordered. Five hundred of them.

> *Henry C. Beecham*
>
> **Rain Made to Order**
> **Success Guaranteed**

He left St. Elmo without a single goodbye, not even to Miss Emmons, and he never came back.

News of his rainmaking success all over the West drifted back to town, as everything drifts back to a railroad town, and people who had known him and his family were continually astonished to hear of his achievements. Not because they didn't believe that rain could be made to order or success guaranteed, but because Hank was a Beecham, and they were luckless, shiftless, worthless, violent, and drunken and always would be.

So it was something of a comedown for the august city fathers to greet Hank at the station, to take him in one of their fine cars to the city's best hotel and put him up as the city's guest. They might not have invited him at all, except that their hour of need had stretched from days into months, month after month without rain, though from every pulpit— Mormon, Methodist, Catholic, Baptist, the African Redeemed Church of the Lamb, the private pulpits of the Chinese— the Almighty was beseeched to send rain to the St. Elmo Valley. Persistently, He declined. St. Elmo wilted. Forage crops that could usually endure the dryness withered; the infant citrus industry puckered up, collapsed; sheep too dumb to seek water dropped beside dried-up troughs; even hogs searching for a bit of forbidden wallow in the city streets (there were ordinances against this) couldn't find three square inches of mud and died where they fell. Every two-bit grass fire aided and abetted by a stiff wind threatened to become an inferno. Prices rose, tempers flared, and the desert sun seared into the flesh and burnt the eyes of everyone in the St. Elmo Valley.

All this in an election year.

CHAPTER TWO

After driving Hank Beecham to the New Town Hotel and showing him to the fine room just opposite that given Signor Federicci, the four escorted him to the Pilgrim Restaurant for lunch. That they took Hank to the Pilgrim testified to their civic commitment to rain. Each of the four men had reason to disapprove of the Pilgrim and its owner, the Widow Douglass. Sid Ferris's aversion to her was rooted in jealousy, because the Pilgrim's heathen Chinese cook was so far superior to anyone he could hire for his hotel's kitchen. Otis McGahey disapproved because Ruth Douglass had hired a Chinese in the first place. Lew Cannon disapproved because the Mormon widow had flouted the church's teachings; she had refused offers of lawful marriage from decent Latter-day Saint men and remained unmarried, an unnatural state for a woman. Worse, she maintained a longstanding friendship with the atheist doctor and allowed her children to listen to his blasphemous notions—and on the Sabbath at that. Weekly, the atheist came to Sunday dinner at her home. Art Whickham detested Ruth Douglass because she was his wife's sister. As unlike Art's wife as a pickle from a poke bonnet, Ruth seldom spoke to her sister, for which Art was grateful, but he prickled under the necessity of being related to a woman who, even if she knew her place, refused to keep it.

"Good afternoon, Art," she greeted him casually. Art was continually nettled by her lack of respect. She was tall and cool and stern as a peach tree in winter.

As the five men, led by Ruth, walked through the Pilgrim, with its high ceiling, starched white curtains, and tables clad in starched white cloths, the lunchtime patrons momentarily hushed—even the Ladies' Culture League, clustered around Signor Federicci. Everyone knew who Hank was and why he'd come, and they regarded him with equal parts of hope and suspicion. When Ruth brought them to their reserved table, Otis McGahey, reflexively sycophantic, asked the Widow Douglass how she managed to maintain the wilting chrysanthemums in the tiny vase.

"I throw the slops on them," Ruth replied, handing each man a menu and leaving.

McGahey flushed. "You see what it's come to?"

"The question is," Sid Ferris demanded, "where is it going to end? That's the question. That's the question we'd better address before we all dry up and blow away. Right, Hank? You wouldn't want to see your own hometown dry up and blow away."

"I wrote you my terms. One thousand dollars per inch of rain."

Sid Ferris broke into a sweat, and Otis McGahey's face took on a crimson cast as he spluttered, "Yes, but, of course, it's not, well, not exactly robbery or anything like that, but, certainly no one could, well, it's definitely exorbitant. I think we could all agree on that."

"Not all of us," Hank replied.

The four fell silent, studying the menu. They recommended everything on it.

Hank did not open his menu. He took out a small bag of tobacco and swiftly rolled himself a cigarette and lit it. The four watched his hands closely; they were long bony hands with slender fingers and huge knuckles, and the flesh on them resembled a patchwork quilt sewn by a lunatic, the scars stitched to one another, each bit of flesh a slightly different color. "I'll have steak, fried eggs, pie, and coffee," said Hank. "That's all I ever eat. I stick to the essentials. I don't fuss. I don't dicker. I'm good at what I do."

"You're sure you can deliver?" asked Art.

"If you're not, I shouldn't be here. If it's not worth a thousand dollars an inch to you, we're wasting time."

"We may be anyway," Lew Cannon muttered. "It might be God's will. We don't want another flood like 1911, when—"

"Now, Hank," Otis interceded jovially, "of course we're sure you can deliver. We know what you did for Santa Rosita. We've followed your career for years. This city, this valley has every confidence in you. Why, you're one of us! That's why we thought, being as we're your own hometown and all, well, we thought your rates might be a little different for St. Elmo."

"I make money making rain. If I don't make money, I don't make rain." A Chinese waiter came up to take their orders, and Hank puffed on his cigarette. "I never knew any one of you to alter your rates for your own hometown."

Art's bank, Sid's commercial enterprises, Otis's legal savvy, and Judge Lew Cannon's guarantee of a friendly court meant that these four were the richest men in St. Elmo. Aside from 'their investments, real estate, and salaries, they were owners of the infant Doradel Fruit Company (Doradel seeming a more modest name than Eldorado) and Empire Lands (a not-so-modest name). Forage crops were grown on Empire's vast acres, and what with the war devastating Europe, these crops could fetch particularly high prices now. They were, in short, the men with the most to lose if the drought continued, and so they shifted their weight uneasily in their chairs, because of course Hank was right: they would not have altered their rates for a band of angels.

"St. Elmo never gave me a thing," Hank continued. "I don't owe this town nothing. One thousand per inch. Like it or lump it. It don't matter to me. It's been a dry year all over the West. I don't hurt for work. I got my methods and I got my price. I don't change neither for no one. I don't dicker. I'm good at what I do." He dropped his cigarette butt into the narrow vase with the mums and cracked the knuckles of his huge hands. "But if you want to wait for God, that's fine with me."

The meal before them, Sid Ferris turned the conversation to the remarkable civic progress of St. Elmo in the twenty years that Hank had been gone. The others contributed proudly, dwelling on the high school, the hospital, the sewer system, the electric streetlights adorning the (mostly) paved streets, along which electric streetcars rattled. Automobiles were so common now, they scarcely spooked the horses. They described the bustle and the refinements of New Town, crowned by Sid's hotel and, Otis declared, "the grandest opera house south of Los Angeles."

"That ain't saying much," Hank replied, using a bit of steak to mop up his eggs. "Doctor Tipton still here?"

Lew Cannon growled, "That atheist?"

"Doctor Lucius Tipton."

"Yes," Otis offered. "Lucius Tipton still lives in his old house. He . . ." But Otis did not continue, as he could only damn with faint praise, and that did not seem the best way of getting Hank Beecham for less than one thousand dollars per inch.

Art Whickham ate in haste. He was a man of few enthusiasms, and food was not one of them. Money was. "Consider this. Consider a wager. You're a gambling man, aren't you, Hank?"

"No. I don't drink. I don't gamble. I don't womanize."

Otis McGahey blushed furiously and glanced around covertly to ascertain if any voters had overheard this egregious breach of good taste.

"Oh," Art continued, "I didn't mean gambling as a vice. Far from it. No indeed, I meant it as a way of looking at the world."

Hank chewed the last of his steak reflectively. "That surprises me, coming from you. Since when did bankers gamble?"

"Every day, Hank. Every penny that goes out of my bank, I gamble on its being returned to me."

"Fourfold," said Hank sourly.

"Be that as it may. I'm a man who likes a little risk. Keeps the juices flowing. Keeps you from getting stale and predictable and too comfortable, if you know what I mean. These gentlemen"—Art gestured graciously to his companions—"they've taken risks. If they hadn't, they wouldn't be where they are today, which is leading this city forward with the twentieth century. What would you say to a professional wager, Hank?"

Hank motioned to the waiter for his pie and rubbed his scarred hands together till they made a rasping sound. "I'd say I didn't know Mormons wagered."

"A *professional* wager. Your skills against our money."

Hank's pale blue eyes flickered. "I make rain. That's all I do."

"God should deliver us from drought," Lew Cannon interjected.

The judge might have gone on, but Art cut him off quickly by asking if Hank had heard that after the 1911 flood, the Army Corps of Engineers had constructed a new dam and reservoir—called the Urquita Reservoir—in the mountains east of town. He went on about the dam's standing for civic progress and a commitment to the future and concluded with a question. "You think you can fill that reservoir, Hank?"

Hank mopped his colorless mustache with a napkin. "How dry is it?"

"Dry."

"Near cracked open and dry as the egg on your plate," Otis added.

Slowly, Art said, "Here's the wager. We'll give you forty-five days. You fill that reservoir and we'll pay you fifty thousand dollars."

McGahey's fork crashed to the floor, and Sid Ferris choked on his coffee. Lew Cannon groaned and paled, and his hands flew to his heart.

"You don't fill it," Art went on, "and you don't get a cent. Like I said, a professional wager. All or nothing. The reservoir filled, fifty thousand dollars. You don't fill it—even if you bring rain—we don't pay you a cent." Art turned to his comrades. "Wouldn't you agree, gentlemen, that it's worth fifty thousand dollars to this valley to have the reservoir filled?"

They recovered slowly and nodded one by one. They were awestruck by the very sound of fifty thousand dollars. All of New Town hadn't cost that much to build. Fifty thousand dollars could outfit an entire army! Fifty thousand impossible dollars! But they were equally intrigued by the prospect of paying nothing at all.

Hank Beecham cracked the knuckles of his patchwork hands. He shaded his eyes as if peering into the sun and the distance, into a clouded future or a near-forgotten past. He rolled himself a cigarette but did not light it. He toyed with it. "Give me sixty days, and five hundred dollars to get started," he said at last. "I'll do it. All or nothing."

"Done!" cried Otis McGahey with a grin and a gavel-like fist brought down on the table.

"Not quite." Hank held up one of his bleached, bony, hairless hands. "You got to abide by my condition. I always work the same way and by the same condition: I get credit for every drop of rain that falls from this very day forward. If it rains tomorrow, it's my rain, no matter what. If it rains afore I lift my hand, it's my rain. If that reservoir fills afore we leave this here table, it's my rain. I win. You owe me."

Otis McGahey gave a lawyerly look to the others. They smiled and nodded knowingly. "Caveat accepted."

The four parted company with Hank Beecham in the lobby of the New Town Hotel, where the Ladies' Culture League was bidding farewell—for the moment—to Signor Federicci, who returned their effusions with equally elaborate promises to meet once again at the home of Signora McGahey that very evening for dinner, when they would settle the details to bring *La Traviata* to St. Elmo in January. Hank pushed past this silken throng and bought a newspaper at the desk. He climbed the stairs to his room.

Once there, he bounced several times on the bed, as though doubting its veracity. Without otherwise taking note of his splendid surroundings, he read the local *Gazette* and beheld the usual round of local events—"Roundhouse Saloon Brawl Injures Five," "St. Elmo High School Debate Team Places Third"—lined up against dreary news of the Great War, European names and places that people in St. Elmo could hardly pronounce, much less envision: Dobrudja, Saloniki, Ancre, villages blasted, earth bloodied, barbed wire festooned with the flesh of the dead, numberless men facing each other in trenches, No Man's Land between them, shooting, gassing, bombing the enemy, each side proclaiming a fight to the finish. War, more war, and nothing but war. Hank perused all this laconically till he found what he was looking for: mention of torrential rains hampering both the Allies and the Hun, sloughing mud into the trenches, where men knee-deep in water jostled with rats. He returned to the front page and "Rainmaker Returns to Valley," a small article noting his long string of successes throughout the West, mentioning that Hank had been born in St. Elmo, and tactfully steering clear of any further discussion of his family.

He closed the paper and went to the desk near the window, where on New Town stationery he wrote orders for chemicals from three different supply houses, one in Buffalo, one in Chicago, and one in St. Louis. He kept his formulas to himself and parceled out his orders so that no one supplier would be able to guess his combinations, much less their proportions. He put his coat on, posted the letters at the desk in the lobby, and asked the freckled young man there the way to the blacksmith's, only to be told that the blacksmith's now styled itself a garage and could be found at the corner of Wesley and Brigham (these street names reflecting the intersection of goodwill between Methodists and Mormons).

Hank took a long roundabout route, looking for the old repair shop with the two rooms above it where his mother had died. But the building had collapsed in the 1911 flood, and only a few gray-green tumbleweeds grew there, rocking back and forth in the desert wind, moaning like new widows. He walked around the empty lot. "Fifty thousand, Ma," he repeated over and over. "For your angel, Ma. Your stone. Rose-colored Italian marble, Ma, to your memory, bigger and better than anything in the whole cemetery, in the whole town." Hank envisioned this angel as a monument to the stubborn pride his mother had instilled in him, to her last words, the single dictum she had lived by: *Never forget.* That was what Eulalie Beecham had taught her youngest, her best beloved son. *Not a dollar or a two-bit piece. Never forget a wrong or a slight. Remember and be damned if you must, but never excuse anything in the name of time.*

At the blacksmith's-cum-garage, Hank ordered four vats the size of copper washtubs made to his specifications, with rings of iron bolted on inside and out. He asked directions to the hardware store, which was just down the street. There, he left an order which took an hour just to write down—

infusing joy in the heart of the owner, who assured Mr. Beecham it would all be attended to. When did he want it? "I'll tell you when," said Hank. "You just get it together." From there, he walked over to the lumberyard near the train station and ordered lumber, building materials, corrugated tin, and piping, to be delivered to an as yet unspecified place on an as yet undesignated date.

Hank Beecham was surprised to go through this town he best remembered as a dusty desert stop-off, nothing to recommend it but the railroad. In the St. Elmo he remembered, only the creak of wooden wagons, the arhythmic thud of horses' hooves had clattered through town. Now, though pedestrians still had to sidestep mounds of drying horse dung, smoky exhaust from motors perfumed the air, and Hank much preferred the streetcar's noisy rattle to a horse's whinny. Even the horses, Hank noted, stupid as they were, wouldn't drink from the public troughs along commercial streets, where the water was scummy and opaque, coated with a thick rind of dust. Everywhere in town, people's eyes followed Hank as he walked or rode the streetcar. No one spoke to him, but everyone knew who he was and why he had come and what he could do.

He came to the shiny red, white, and blue pole of a barbershop, rubbed his jaw and the wispy fringe at his neck. He stepped in before he saw the barber was a black man. All the patrons were white and all the barbers were black, blood relations of the proprietor, Grief Bowers.

Grief was the youngest of Nana Bowers' fifteen children. His odd name his mother had explained by saying that after fifteen children, she had run out of everything but grief. Nana Bowers had indeed borne her share of loss, sorrow, and pain since she had accompanied the famous Mormon scout Madison Whickham, who with five of his thirteen wives had settled St. Elmo in 1850. Nana was a girl then, the slave of Madison Whickham. But it was not true that she had run out of everything but grief. She had not run out, for instance, of shrewdness and industry, which she also managed to instill in her considerable tribe of children and their many descendants as well. Nor had she run out of native ingenuity. Beginning in St. Elmo's earliest pioneer days (when Nana compounded ink made of nutgalls), up through the years when boot blacking, mouse deterrent, and green salve for wounds were in demand, and into a more prosperous era (when she made up oatmeal soap, powdered lemonade, and hair restoratives and ran a Turkish bath in a Mormon town), there was nothing Nana Bowers could not turn to profit. Moreover, everything Mrs. Bowers concocted enhanced lives, made them cleaner and more pleasurable. The formulas did not die with her. Even now, Grief used Nana Bowers' Famous Italian Beard Enhancer on Hank Beecham's hard jaw before he began to shave him.

Unrelaxed, Hank sat in the chair and watched Grief in

the mirror, remembering Jeremiah Beecham's drunken demand to know how it was a black family could prosper in a white man's town. Watching the affable efficient Grief in his pleasant barbershop, the answers, even all these years later, were painfully obvious.

"There you go, Mr. Beecham," said Grief, whisking the white apron off him, dusting his neck with a brush.

"How'd you know my name?" asked Hank, exchanging his first words with anyone in the shop.

"You're the rainmaker, Mr. Beecham. Everyone knows you're here." Grief splashed a dash of gingery cologne on his hands and was about to apply it to Hank's face when Hank rose out of the chair. Grief wiped the cologne on his own apron. "You need a shoeshine, Mr. Beecham? My son be back from school any minute now. Our own polish. Best shoeshine in California. Right here in St. Elmo."

"You 'member me from before?" demanded Hank. "From a long time ago?"

"No, Mr. Beecham. I read the paper." Grief met Hank's gaze evenly.

He handed the barber a coin and gave them all, white and black, a merciless look before inquiring, "Which way to Doctor Tipton's house?"

"You walking or taking the streetcar?"

"Walking."

Grief Bowers gave him directions, and his son, just returned from school, held the barbershop door open for Hank Beecham as Grief shook out the white apron smartly and called his next customer up by name.

CHAPTER FOUR

I lock up the office because—unless someone decides to die or get themselves born in the next twelve hours—I reckon my day's work is done. As always, I wash up, go on through to my study, and light the lamps. Don't suppose I'll ever get used to thinking, *Turn on the light,* though I have electricity now. I'll probably always say, *Light the lamps,* and I do say so, now, to Blanche hanging there behind my desk chair, skeletally suspended and companionable in her fashion, downright chatty when I tilt my chair back and rattle her bones. She and I are about to take up the pleasures of the out-of-town papers with a shot of Burning Bush Whiskey when I hear a knock at the door and I find there a tall, spare, blasted-looking man, hat pulled low. No one I know, but as a doctor, you get used to strangers showing up.

"I come to pay you," he says.

"Well, never let it be said I turned away a debtor. Come in. Pay me for what?"

"You don't 'member me, do you?"

"I recognize botched-up hands when I see them." I took the man's hands in my own. "I hope you haven't come to pay me for these. I hope these aren't my handiwork."

He wrested his hands back. "They weren't. I come to pay you for my mother, Eulalie Beecham."

"Oh yes! Beecham the rainmaker! I read all about your coming back here in the *Gazette*. You used to own a repair shop over on—"

"I never owned nothing in this town. I still don't own nothing, but that's my choice. I make good money now. Real good. I got your fee with interest. I got the money for my sister too. Virginia Beecham."

I bring him into the study, which is book lined and smells of smoke and print, and I motion him to a seat in an overstuffed chair across from me. All over my desk, there's out-of-town newspapers and open books. He lowers himself in a deliberate fashion, as if not trusting the chair. I sit back, introduce him to Blanche, and finally I say, "That was all a long time ago, Mr. Beecham."

"Hank will do. Twenty years for Ma. More for Virginia."

He pulled his hat from his head.

"Well, Hank, tell me how it is the city fathers finally gave up on God and turned to a rainmaker."

"Ask them yourself. I take the job or I don't. I can say this, though. The difference 'tween me and God is that God works for free."

"When He works," I offered.

"And when He don't, He can't be bought."

"You can?"

"I come dear. Fifty thousand. That's the wager I struck with them. All or nothing. I fill the reservoir, I get fifty thousand dollars. I don't fill it and I don't get a penny."

Fifty thousand? It took me a bit to recover from the very notion. *Fifty thousand dollars!* I'm not sure I did recover, but I managed to ask if he'd seen the reservoir yet. He hadn't. "You got a lot of confidence to make that kind of wager before you have a look."

"I'm good at what I do." He cracked his knuckles. "Fifty thousand," he said, rolling the sum off his tongue as though it had flavor and succulence.

I opened a desk drawer and pulled out two cigars, offered one to Hank.

"I'm a cigarette man," he informed me.

"Cigarettes are nothing but a practice. Now, a good cigar"—I held it up to my ear and listened to it crinkle—"that's an art."

"I don't hold with art. Only science."

From behind my blazing match, I regarded this grizzled visitor whose intensity and conviction belied the emptiness of his blue eyes. "Well, I believe in science. Science always aspires to truth."

"Truth don't interest me, but I always held with science, even when I was fixing sewing machines. You seen one sewing machine, you seen 'em all. But a rainstorm, that's true science. You get something new and glorious with every one. I stand there and the rain pours down on me and I know I done it. It's glorious, thunder and lightning wrestling over the sky. The wrath of it," he added, drawing out his bag of tobacco and papers, expertly rolling a cigarette. "With science, I know what God must of felt like. If I held with God. Which I don't."

I took the bottle of Burning Bush Whiskey from the bottom drawer. "Can I offer you a drink?"

"I don't drink."

"I see." I burbled a little Burning Bush into a glass and remembered that Jeremiah Beecham drank. Horace Beecham drinks. Earl Beecham at age eighteen is already dancing toward delirium tremens. "Well, you been spared your family's curse."

"Pa ruint everything he touched. 'Cept for me. I 'scaped 'cause of Ma. Ma and luck."

"Luck's like rain," I said. "Sometimes it just comes and

sometimes you got to make it yourself."

Hank Beecham snorted in what might once have been a laugh. "I made my luck, all right, but it goes to show how there's no 'counting for how you come by it. My old man, he give me my luck. That blabbering drunken fool. He'd get so drunk he'd piss hisself afore he could get up off the chair— or the floor. But he give me ideas. Them and a lot of bruises, black eyes, and a coupla cracked ribs now and then. It was the War the old man loved better than anything 'cept drink. The War was the happiest days of his life." Hank glanced at the Western Front headlines of the *Chicago Tribune*. "He'd of loved this war too. It would of suited him."

"Sheer waste, this European war, squandering, sickening, mad waste."

"Men who love war don't give a pig's whistle about waste. Battle's all that matters. My old man, for all his waving the Bonnie Blue Flag, he didn't give a rat's ass for the South. He made all that up later. All but the battles. He didn't make those up. He loved 'em. He'd crack a bottle and didn't matter a tick to him if there was anyone round to listen or not, he'd flap on about the rain and fire, the smoke, the shot, the shell, bullets buzzing overhead like a swarm of hornets. I heard it all my life. I got so's I knew every dead Reb, every bone-blasted Yankee." Hank smoked, drawing it deep into his lungs and letting it out slowly. "The old man'd go on and on, how God sent the rain after every battle to wash the dead clean and make the living suffer so's they'd wish they was dead, washing over Reb and Union alike, knowing no loyalty, bogging all the supply wagons, soaking all the rations, rotting their clothes, pounding on their wounds, artillery wheel-deep in mud, wet fuses, wet powder, wet cornmeal. The bigger the battle, the more rain would follow. It never failed. Pa said it was the rain cost the South the Battle of Shiloh. The smoke and the rain. Firing at each other so close like that, Reb and Yank, they couldn't see where to aim for the smoke. It was a wall of fire, Pa said, a wall of flame, and then the woods all round caught fire. The wounded burnt to death. Pa said you could hear 'em. Pa could still hear 'em, even after we moved here." He plucked a bit of tobacco from his tongue and studied it.

"He fight in the Hornet's Nest?"

"You know Shiloh, Doctor?"

"I know of it. I had an uncle who fought there. My mother's brother. Lost his leg at Shiloh."

"Union man?"

"Yes. But after Shiloh, they knew—both sides knew—it was no ninety-day jig they were about, everything to be settled up quick and everyone go home. It was the same thing with this war. In 1914, people thought the soldiers would all be home before Christmas. Now, look at this." I pointed to the Chicago paper. "How long they been fighting at the Somme? Months. No victory. Just defeat."

"Well, Shiloh was both, victory and defeat, in them two days, and there shouldn't of been no second day at that. That Sunday night, Pa and all his victorious Rebs, they're looting Sherman's camps, eating Yankee cheese and drinking Yankee wine, bayoneting pictures of Yankee sweethearts, while from the river, the big guns fire, huge shells every fifteen minutes. Don't no one sleep that night. The rain and the guns. Rain and guns. Pa used to say he'd moved to a dry place so's he could get away from the rain and the mis'ry, which was the very thing he loved and never would leave, never let go of. Sometimes, he'd hunker hisself into a squat and weep, say the rain coming down after battles was God's mercy. Then sometimes"—Hank opened his hand, palm up, dropped his ashes into it, closed his fingers over the cinders—"he'd fire hisself up into a rage and declare it God's undying wrath. I heard it all my life. Rain to follow fire. God's wrath. When I quit believing in God, I got to wondering, questioning—if God didn't send that rain, who did?"

I looked at him expectantly.

"I tried to reason it out like you do a sewing machine, but you can't toggle and mend such a question. You got to open it up. You got to lay science like a grid over history, push down hard and see what comes up. I could see that God hadn't nothing to do with it a'tall. It was the invention of gunpowder. Five hundred years ago, give or take. Firepower, Doctor. Rain follows a firepower battle just as sure as death and destruction. Men brought the rain with their guns, their cannons, their shot and shell. They did it without knowing or thinking what they was about."

"So," I offered, "you figured if men did it, then science could duplicate it."

"That's what come up through the grid," he said, threading his long tattered fingers one over the other. He regarded his hands studiously, then released them. "I knew I could make rain, and I done it. Not right away, but I done it. Combined precision with instinct. Made my rain and made my own luck, though it was too late to do Ma any good. Best woman who ever drew breath, Ma was. If she'd lived, she'd be rich, sitting in one of them big comfortable homes on Silk Stocking Row right now, good fire, good shoes, warm clothes. She'd be living alongside the Whickhams and McGaheys and the Cannons. She'd have a servant and a motorcar and never a fret." He paused almost wistfully. "So would Martha."

"Martha?" I sipped my Burning Bush.

"Martha Emmons. My wife."

The Burning Bush tangled going down, and I choked. "You married Miss Emmons?"

"Didn't you know that?" Hank gave a quick lick to the palm of his hand and put his cigarette out there. "I thought sure Martha would of told folks she was leaving St. Elmo to get married."

I shook my head, trying to remember, to picture Martha Emmons at all. "We never knew any such thing, only that one day, the principal walks past Miss Emmons's classroom and the children are fighting and throwing things and some of them are crying and a few bloody noses and there's dirty words all over the blackboard and no Miss Emmons in sight. Herschel Petrey, head of the Board of Education himself, went round to Sister Whitworth's boardinghouse and came back with the word that Miss Emmons had left a week's rent on her bureau and she was gone. Not another word's been heard of her since."

"She divorced me."

Divorce is rarer than rain in St. Elmo, and my face must have showed it.

"She stuck with me long as she could stand it. Then she divorced me. She could of just left me, but Martha was tidy like that. Wanted it all done up proper. She got me for desertion. She knew it weren't the truth. I never deserted Martha. She deserted me. She knew I was a rainmaker when she married me. She knew the life I lived, would always live. Still," Hank shrugged, "she must of thought it would all be different. Curtains at the window. Flowers at the door. I didn't want none of that. Never have."

"What did you want?"

Hank's pale blue eyes rested on Blanche, or some point in the far distance. "I come about the fees for Ma and Virginia."

"Forget it."

"I don't forget nothing, Doctor. Fifty dollars. That oughta cover it with interest. Twenty-five for Ma and the same for Virginia."

"Fifty dollars is out of the question! I won't hear of it."

"Ma would of paid you for Virginia herself, but there wasn't enough to buy millet after Virginia run off. Pa had to sell the bed so's he could drink. I'm gonna pay it, Doctor—the fee and more. It ain't the money. You done my family a service. Twice. You come to Ma's side when she was dying, you eased her through that awful pain. You come to her funeral even if we hadn't paid you. I respect that. Don't know that I'd of done the same, but I respect it in another man. You're the only man I respect in this spineless, puny-ass, piss-hearted town, and I come to make good my family's debts."

I puffed thoughtfully on my cigar. "Why didn't you pay me when your mother died? I ask only as a matter of curiosity. Why wait all these years?"

"Time means nothing to me. I never forget, not a debt nor disgrace, 'sides I knew there'd be money one day. But after I buried Ma, all I wanted was to get shut of this town, to get away from Pa and Horace. Pa killed Ma just as sure as he killed Virginia."

"Virginia's dead too?"

"Prob'ly. I been all over the West and northern Mexico these twenty-some years, and I finally give up looking for her. Prob'ly she's better off dead."

"She might have married and changed her name. She was just a girl when she left."

"Fifteen. Soon as she was strong enough to walk, soon as she could sneak out and saddle up that nag, Virginia was gone."

I scrutinized the man across from me, the man with hands so hardened he could put a cigarette out in them without wincing, and I thought about his sister, Virginia Beecham, writhing with pain, legs spread, cascading a river of blood between her white thighs, her mother stanching it efficiently, evincing no emotion.

"What are you going to do now?" Eulalie Beecham demands.

I hold the girl and give her the chloroform, and she takes it like a salvation wafer and sinks back on the bed. "Whatever's necessary," I reply.

"Whatever's necessary for what?" asks Eulalie Beecham, who might once have been a good-looking woman but was now frayed and tattered— parched skin, hair, hands, clothes, all of it but the eyes. The blue eyes were clear and hard as agates.

"Whatever's necessary to complete what your daughter has begun."

"She says she wants to die, Doctor."

"She's not going to die. Not if I can save her."

So I saved her. Saved Virginia Beecham so nine days later she could take every penny that hardscrabble desert-dog family ever had, every penny the old man hadn't drunk up, every penny Eulalie had pinched and skimmed and hoarded in that leather envelope she hid behind the lard can, take that and their only horse and bolt beyond the reach of her old man or the law or time itself. I saved her, and while I worked in the blood-and-tissue-clotted mess Virginia had made of her own innards, my heart broke for a girl who had done this to herself, who preferred near-death and inconceivable pain over conventional dishonor. I say to Eulalie Beecham when I'm done, when I'm washing the blood off my hands and boiling instruments, I say, "I suppose her father's out with a horsewhip looking for the boy."

Eulalie takes the basin of water I'd reddened with her daughter's blood and throws it out the door. "Virginia's pa is out in the barn. Drunk. Dead drunk. Dead if we was real lucky."

I say nothing, just write out my instructions and what to look for in case infection should develop, leave those and some iron pills I'd compounded myself on the table and tell Eulalie Beecham to bring Virginia to my office in ten days' time. Then, soon as I'd spoken, I knew Eulalie would never march her daughter into town, not after an operation like this. "Never mind," I say. "I'll come back out in ten days. I'll check her then. If you see infection coming on, anything like it, send one of your boys into town to get me."

Eulalie Beecham went to the shelf and moved the lard can and pulled out a leather envelope. She starts to count out her coins, but I tell her don't. "Later," I say. "You pay me when I come back out in ten days."

Eulalie puts the money back in the envelope and moves the lard can back over it and offers me her toughened hand, like we were horse traders who had just struck an agreeable deal. "I'll never forget this, Doctor. Never."

"I don't remember you out there that night," I said, leaning back on my desk chair, rattling Blanche. "I think it was your brother Horace who came to fetch me."

"Ma banished me to the loft of the barn and said I wasn't to let Pa know I was there and just stay put and be silent till she come for me. Me and Virginia was the babies of the family. She didn't have no use for the others. So I did like Ma said, I lay in the loft and listened to the old drunk whimper and shriek hisself blind. I heard Horace come in and rouse him. Horace says, Come on, Pa. Let's go out and find the boy who done this to Virginia. Let's go get that boy and whup him, Pa." Hank released a laugh not natural or easy. "What a fool that Horace was. There wasn't no boy. Even I knew who done that to Virginia."

My hand tightened round the glass of Burning Bush, and I drank. That was a hard one to swallow. "So it was not conventional dishonor that drove Virginia Beecham to ream out her own insides," I said at last. "No wonder she wanted to die."

"Well, they're both beyond pain now, Ma and Virginia. Nothing can ever hurt them again. Ma was plenty hurt. Beat up. Often. Took the strap for me too, when she could. And Virginia, well, it was as you say, Doctor, she wanted to die." He looked toward Blanche and the past, seeing perhaps in Blanche's bones the years between him and his mother, his sister. "Ma was glad when Virginia got away. She couldn't say it, natcherly, didn't dare to, neither of us, but we was both glad Virginia 'scaped. Ma was always telling me, You leave too, Henry. You leave, Henry. Soon as you can get away from here, you leave. But I'd never leave Ma there with those two. Just walk out and leave her there with Pa and Horace? What kind of man you take me for, Ma?" He seemed to address the question to Blanche.

"You weren't a man then. You were just a boy."

Hank shrugged. "I wasn't a fool. Even then, I wasn't a fool."

"Fools are born, not made," I said. "If you're not a fool from birth, then you got a hope in this world."

Hank Beecham stood. He put fifty dollars on the desk in front of me, and again I declined. "You come to my mother in her dying and you saved Virginia's life. You never told no one, neither, about what Virginia done to herself. Gossip moves like brush fire through St. Elmo, and it would of come back to us if you had. You never told a soul what you saw there that night. What you knew."

"Gallstones, man! I don't betray my patients!"

Hank pushed the money toward me. "Like I said, you're the only man in St. Elmo I got any respect for. This town is nothing but a gathering of greasy humbugs. But you, you're a professional, Doctor, a man of science, like me. I'll give you some advice, one man of science to another. You'd best nail down everything you don't want to float away. You'd best build yourself an ark, because when I'm done with my rain, when I work my rain this time, it's gonna be the finest work I ever done, and this town's gonna look like Lake Tahoe."

I shuddered involuntarily. I have seen my fill of flood. Back in 1911.

Ruth and I, wet clear through, watching while they dragged the drowned from the river, pulled their bodies out of the train that had gone down with the bridge. Ruth and I helpless, dumb, clinging to each other in the pelting rain. I could see what—no, who—they were next pulling from the water, and I knew that I alone must see this, Ruth must not, that this wet vision would sear her eyes forever after. Just then, Tom Lance comes up on horseback, says Afton sent him to take Ruth home. I push Ruth toward that horse and Tom hoists her behind him and I slap the horse's flank. And then I turn back to the river, where they are securing ropes to the body of young Eden Douglass in her wine-colored suit— Ruth's eldest daughter, sweet Eden—and they slowly pull her body out of the flood, out of the raging current, and into the rain, and put her, lifeless, into my soaking arms.

I said drily, "Maybe you'd best be careful, Hank. We already been swept out to sea in 1911. We don't need that again."

"You need rain. They brung me to make rain. I will give them rain."

"For a man who doesn't believe in God, you sound downright biblical."

"I'm good at what I do," replied Hank Beecham, cracking

his knuckles, taking his leave, and stepping out into the tinder-dry night.

A day or two after he came to my office to pay, with interest, a debt a quarter-century past due, I heard how Hank Beecham left the New Town Hotel, told them to hold his room, and walked, carrying his single satchel, to the Feed and Seed. He ordered some provisions and a saddle (used), and then he said he wanted to buy a horse and they should find him one, a reliable hardworking horse, nothing skittish or showy. He said he'd pay cash money and wouldn't dicker. Well, you can just imagine how many horses were suddenly up for sale, and one was found for him. At Goodlove's Dry Goods, Hank bought a fry pan, coffeepot, coffee, eggs, lard, and flour, and then he got on that horse and he left town and no one saw him for about two weeks. But when he comes back down from the Urquita Reservoir (I heard this from Tom Lance, Afton's husband, who was getting his hair cut at Bowers' Barber Shop then), Hank Beecham looked wild-eyed as an Old Testament prophet. Tom Lance said he looked like Moses come down from the mountains having seen what the rest of us couldn't endure. I asked Tom: You think he brought down the Word too, maybe writ on Golden Tablets? But it did not wash as funny. Tom's a Mormon, and so Golden Tablets just aren't funny-fodder. In any event, Tom and the rest of them at Bowers', they watched Hank kind of slide off that horse (which also looked the worse for the experience) and leave it in the street like it would comb, curry, and feed itself. That horse could have dropped dead and Hank would not have cared or noticed.

I heard later, from a few of the men who were in the New Town Bar that night, that Hank came downstairs about six hours later, and finding the dining room closed, he went to the bar and ordered his usual meal. The men there, a good-natured lot (unless one of them is running for office), introduced themselves, offered to buy him a drink, tried to jaw him up about the drought, about the rain, about the bet and the reservoir, maybe the war in Europe and the world in general.

When the steak and eggs arrive, Hank tells them he can't breathe. *You'll have to leave*, he tells them without a morsel of fellow feeling, *you're taking up my oxygen. I'm good at what I do, and that's all you need to know of me.* They fan out, away from him, the way I see it, like some ebbing tide of humanity, leaving him beached all alone there in the New Town Bar.

Next day, everyone heard how he went to the lumber-yard and told them there'd be deliveries coming from the hardware, the dry goods, and the blacksmith's, and that the whole of it should be loaded up and delivered to a patch of ground above the Urquita Reservoir. He said they should be ready at dawn and he would lead them up.

The lumberman says he's heard that some of this order is dynamite, blasting caps, and gunpowder, and he don't want the responsibility and so on, his objections mostly having to do with the state of the road up to the reservoir, how it's steep and narrow and his trucks won't do it, can't, with that heavy of a load, and besides he doesn't have that many trucks, and the size of the vats, the steel piping for the towers, and on and on. This man was just full of every reason why he couldn't oblige. Hank listens to him with the patience of a man hearing out the begats and begots, but finally he just halts this man, saying real clear and slow, *Then don't use the trucks. You got mules in this town, don't you? You got wagons. Use mules and wagons.* Then Hank says that famous American word, not Life, Liberty, nor the Pursuit of anything in particular, but Cash. *Cash,* says Hank. And behold, the magic works yet again, and the lumberman agrees to find the mules and wagons. Hank adds that along with all this, he wants white men for teamsters, but he also wants three or four Chinese who don't speak much English or read it, Chinese who are willing to work up there for a couple of weeks. He said he'd pay them a dollar a day. The man at the lumberyard said he knew white men who would work for that. Hank Beecham said, *No. I want the Chinese.* And of course, with two bits' worth of brains, you could see he wants the Chinese because they *don't* read English, they don't speak it, and they won't know what Hank's about.

From the lumberyard, Hank walks to Goodlove's Dry Goods, where he pays cash for his already-placed order, enough supplies to outfit an army: buckets and shovels and rubber boots and goggles and workingman's gloves, a whole armada of measuring spoons, a battalion of tins and ladles, a flotilla of scoops and long-handled wooden spoons, a dozen pokers. He bought out Goodlove's stock of matches—that's right, bought him out of matches. I heard this from Ruth's youngest boy, Mason. He works for Goodlove Saturdays and after school. Hank bought flour, lard, eggs, coffee, strong salted bacon, and rice (this must have been for the Chinese). Hank told Goodlove to deliver it all to the lumberyard so it could go up with the wagons, the mules, the white teamsters, and the Chinese. Then he goes back to the blacksmith's and tells him to take the vats he'd ordered to the same place. Then he went to the hardware, told them to send it all over to the lumberyard. Then he went to see Art Whickham for his money, the five hundred dollars cash.

Like everyone else in this town, I heard about how Hank just busted in on Art, not minding the girl out front of his office with her typing machine, not hearing her protest over and over that Mr. Whickham couldn't be disturbed, hearing apparently only the crack and flint of his own knuckles, Hank Beecham walked right into Art Whickham's office. Who does he see there besides Art? His own brother, Horace. Hank hadn't laid eyes on Horace since Eulalie's funeral, and never had seen Horace's boy, Earl, though I doubt he had any trouble recognizing Earl as kin. Earl was all Beecham, like he'd sprung full blown from the Beecham men with no mother at all. No one could even remember Earl's mother. (So lifeless was Mrs. Horace that when she died, neither her husband nor her son knew it. They put her in their wagon and brought her into town to the hospital, and the doctor there directed them to move right along to the morgue. She'd been gone for hours. Days, maybe. Personally, given what I know of the Beechams, I think there should have been an autopsy on Mrs. Horace, an inquiry anyway, but in this county, coroner's an elected office, so he needs no more medical skill than the ability to raise up a hand, and if it falls back down, pronounce the person dead and call his relatives.) Mrs. Horace had lived and died making no dent in the world, and her only child, Earl, was his grandfather all over again, just like Jeremiah, a swaggerer, a bully drunk, a fool sober.

Hank left the door to Art's private sanctum open so everyone in the bank that day (and soon everyone in town) heard Horace Beecham cry out with wonderment about how good it was to see his long-lost brother. Horace embraces him. Hank has not the barest civility, like, *It's good to see you, Horace.* Says nothing to Horace at all. Just nods.

Horace, now, has plenty to say. He goes on and on about how Hank's come to save the Beecham family honor, to save the St. Elmo Valley from drought and despair, to save Shiloh and make it prosper. How the Beechams would finally get some respect from this town, and how even Art Whickham knew it, why else was Art Whickham giving him three months' grace on his mortgage?

When Hank hears this, he says to Art Whickham, *This true?* And Art says, why, yes, he was giving Horace ninety days' grace on the overdue payments, doing it as a personal favor to Hank to show what faith he has in the rainmaker's abilities. Hank asks Art the figure that was in arrears. Art tells him and then Hank turns to Horace and says, *I ain't paying it, Horace. You got your three months from Whickham, maybe, that's 'tween you and him. I ain't paying a cent on that land. I'll never put a penny towards Shiloh.* Then Hank shows his own brother the door, saying he can't abide fools. His brother and his nephew, Earl, they get the git-goodbye, and after they leave,

Hank asks Art for his money and says he's got one more condition for his work.

This showed up in the *Gazette* the next day, a notice boxed up on the front page right between news of the Battle of the Somme and an announcement for Danderine Hair Polish, available only at Bowers' Barber Shop. It says that Hank Beecham will brook no interference. None. No meddling. No one is to come to the site where he is working. If so much as a truant schoolboy shows up out there, the bet is off. No rain. It's a grim announcement followed by assurances and warnings from all the local officials, the mayor and the county sheriff on down, that St. Elmo will respect Hank's wishes. Too much is at stake not to.

Next morning, dawn, Hank, the white teamsters, the three Chinese, five wagons, five teams of mules all leave town and head up to the foothills and the dam and reservoir. The teamsters, wagons, and mules come back a few days later, but that's the last we see of the Chinese and Hank Beecham.

For weeks after that, from the white linen of the Pilgrim Restaurant to the brass rail at the New Town Bar to the spittoons and sawdust of the Roundhouse Saloon, you hear nothing but talk of the rainmaker, and as three hundred and twenty, three hundred and thirty days have passed without rain, you hear nothing but complaints. Next thing you read in the *Gazette* is the city declares they will ration water. Starting

Monday, every household may draw one gallon for each individual in that household, and they are to make that one gallon last all day for all purposes, washing, cooking, cleaning, everything. (It had been months since the city insisted we all take but one bath a week, one tub of water to suffice for everyone in the household.) You can just imagine how those one-gallon jugs began to look to the people of St. Elmo. Probably heathens before their household gods couldn't have looked on those objects with any more reverence, longing, or fervor. No one was exempted. Not the very young, not the very old. The city hospital, I think they might have got a reprieve, but in the city jail, the prisoners, being lesser humanity, didn't get their gallon, but only a quart. People in this town came to say the word *water* as you might once have said *love* or *honor*, like it had a substance and meaning altogether beyond the word itself.

Fortunately, it also meant we were forbidden to use water in our whiskey. One night, I am in the New Town Hotel having a short whiskey at the bar, and not far from me, I hear Otis McGahey holding court (so to speak), addressing the voters there, with Sid Ferris right behind him, and the two of them blaming not God or nature for what's come to pass (or hasn't), but Hank Beecham.

"Beecham made us bet with a single caveat," says Otis, using his best lawyerly voice, "that he should get credit for every drop of rain. I ask you, gentlemen, I say to you: credit for what? Where is this rain? I demand to know: where is this rain? Does he want credit for making our wives and daughters . . . ?" Otis breaks off, and it's clear he was about to say something about not being able to bathe properly, and (since almost everyone gathered around him had wives and daughters) he couldn't think how to say this without suggesting naked respectable women standing before empty tubs. So Sid Ferris steps smartly to his rescue and throws in some muddled thoughts on caveats and credit and finishes up with a couple of biblical quotes, which I figure him to have got from Lew Cannon.

I amble over to them, whiskey in my hand. "What is there to complain about?" I say to Otis and Sid and whoever else wants to listen. "You made a bet with Beecham. All or nothing. He fills the reservoir or you don't pay him a cent. You don't lose a thing."

Otis McGahey has the kind of skin no politician should be cursed with, always blushing and paling and blushing again. He blushes now and says, "Beecham set up out there nearly a month ago. We, the people of the St. Elmo Valley, we're waiting. Where is our rain?"

"You thinking of calling in someone else?" I ask.

"There isn't anyone else."

"Then the choice is clear before you. You wait for Hank Beecham to bring the rain or you wait for God. Personally, I'd put my money on Hank Beecham."

The next day, early, before dawn comes slouching over the eastern mountains, I hear a knock at my door. I pull on my pants and suspenders, guessing it to be a frazzled husband with word of his pregnant wife, but it's Hank Beecham who steps in, inviting me to join him at a hash house near the station for breakfast. "My chemicals come in," he says, "but I got to wait for the depot to open afore I can collect them." He said he had sent the Chinese back to town yesterday.

I look outside into the dark. There's no horse. Nothing. It's as if Hank Beecham had casually collected his personal molecules, called upon them to convene here at my door.

"Did you walk down from the reservoir?"

"I rode that damn fool horse, but I left it at the train sta-tion, used my own two feet to come up here. Can't trust nothing with four feet. Can't trust 'em at all."

Talk of the horse seemed to unsettle him, and he went on, slurring the animal kingdom and horses in particular, while I reckoned up the trouble he would have had getting off that mountain at night. "You did those narrow roads in the dark?"

"No. I come down yesterday." A look of such acute cha-grin crossed his face that I thought maybe gastritis had set in. "I been to Shiloh. I spent the night at Shiloh."

"You went to see Horace and Earl?"

"I don't know what I went to see," he replied grimly.

As we drove to the depot, the Flyer elicited from Hank a modest sort of enthusiasm. He asked me all sorts of ques-tions, how fast it would go, things I could answer, and a lot of ratio-and-revolutions questions I couldn't. Hank admired automobiles, declared them altogether superior to horses, which needed constant tending, feeding, fussing, sheltering, and then they got sick or injured and had to be shot and then buried or burned. "An automobile, now," Hank surmised, "an automobile runs smooth and reliable, just like a sewing machine with wheels. And if it don't, you can just replace the parts and you'll never have to bury it. If I was ever to be a man who owned something 'sides what I carry in this satchel—which I'm not—I can tell what that something would be."

"What's that?"

"One of them Dodge trucks. I hear Pershing's using Dodge trucks down in Chihuahua chasing after Pancho Villa. I once made rain for a Mormon rancher down in Chihuahua, and you never saw such rough land. Any truck that can do that, that would be a truck worth having."

We got to the hash house, open this early for railroad men, and Hank ordered steak, eggs, pie, and coffee. I did the same. I asked what he had found at Shiloh. I didn't ask what he was looking for, because I didn't want to move in too close and take up his oxygen.

"Shouldn't of gone. Ma and me, we never went back to Shiloh, once we 'scaped. Shouldn't of gone back now. Don't know why I did." He sounded annoyed with himself. "The house is still blowing away, splinter by splinter. They got greased paper in the windows, no more glass. No barn. Don't need the barn anyway. Horace and Earl got no animals, 'cept for the chickens. Horace, he was so beside hisself to see me, he was going to kill the fatted chicken because the prodigal'd returneth." Hank's lips curled with derision. "But him and Earl, they were eating ashcake like Pa made during the War, cornmeal, grease, and salt, wrapped in paper and stuck in the ashes till it cooked. They weren't even scraping the paper off to eat it. I told Horace, I don't eat nothing but steak, eggs, pie, and coffee. I stick to the essentials."

"Well, in his own way, probably Horace sticks to the essentials. His essentials are liquid, but he does no harm, not that I've seen."

"He does no good either."

"Earl's the bad one," I observed. "Just eighteen and I've sewed him up twice at the jail after a brawl. Someday, he'll push another man too far and he'll get killed."

"Earl needs a war. He'd be happy with a war. Like Pa."

"Well, he's in luck then. He can go over to Europe and fight the Hun."

"I didn't say he was brave."

The slatternly girl brought our coffee, and Hank took a long swill of his. I lifted mine to my lips, but it was scalding and I couldn't drink. "At least if he fought the Hun, Earl would have his own stories," I reflected, "and wouldn't be clinging to his granddaddy's War, now half a century past."

A fugitive chuckle escaped from deep in Hank's chest. "Oh, Pa could do Chickamauga so's it was real close, so's the bullets whined right through the privy as you sat there. He could do General Cleburne so's you could hear his Irish brogue, smell the smoke from his pipe. To hear Pa tell it, he and Old Pat fought side by side right up to the end. Keep Pa misty for a couple of hours just gutting that story and putting it on to fry. Like a fish. He'd fry that story like a fish." Hank shook his head and might have smiled. "So, natcherly, while I'm there, Horace and Earl had to drink to General Cleburne and all his battles, and to Pa and his battles, and to Pa's having killed the Union general at Shiloh. They done Pa one better in that story."

"One better than what?"

"Well, Pa didn't kill the Union general hisself. It was more like, what you might say, providence. As Pa told it, twenty thousand guns firing, bullets in a swarm overhead, blasting, laying waste to every tree from Shiloh Branch to the Tennessee River, the shrieks of the wounded, the horses dying, and just then, a Union general rides up on his charger, sword flashing in the sunlight, about to cleave Pa's head in half like a melon, when *bang*! A bullet strikes that Union general neat. Through the forehead. He falls dead at Pa's feet. Pa takes the Enfield rifle from the corpse's hand and uses the general's own sword to cut off his buttons and epaulettes. Then Pa rides the general's horse back into battle."

"Sword in one hand," I ask, "epaulettes in the other?"

Hank savored his coffee for a minute. "Well, you wonder what would make a man cut the buttons off a corpse while the battle's raging everywhere, don't you?"

"Maybe the battle wasn't raging. Maybe it was over and they were plundering the dead, looting," I said bluntly. "Only a fool would go into battle, buttons in one hand, epaulettes in the other." The girl brought our breakfasts.

Hank paused, coughed, as though chewing on some gristle of a thought. "I should of reasoned that out a long time ago. Don't know why I didn't. Pa, he was in the high command of liars. Anyway, they're long gone, the buttons, sword, all of 'em long pawned. But while I was out there yesterday, Horace worked hisself into a lather, and Earl too. Earl was gulping tears for the family honor and all dandered up, raging about the sword being sold from its place of pride above the pawnshop counter. If you was a laughing man, Doctor, your chin would of scraped your shinbones to hear 'em both frothing and weeping and carrying on for the Beechams." Hank fell on his eggs with something like gusto. "Then I made the mistake of saying I'd buy the Enfield. The rest of it was trash, but a good Enfield rifle, that still might be worth having."

"Why was that a mistake?"

"Because Horace, then he was desperate to find me something I would buy. Something from the past. He leaves me there with Earl and comes back finally with this pair of boots in hand, women's boots. Ma's own boots, he says. He wanted me to have them. To pay for them. He said he saved Ma's boots all these years because no other woman could fill 'em. Says all this like he loved her." Hank sliced his steak, fat and all, into neat quarter-inch ribbons. "They weren't Ma's boots. Too big. They must of belonged to Horace's wife. Ma was real little. You must remember her."

He said this to me not in an inquiring sort of way, like people do when they already know the answer and want only your confirmation. He said it with a tincture of hope: I *must* remember Eulalie Beecham, I must because no one else would. I said I did. Remembered her well. She wasn't little, though. She was stooped and thin, wind toughened and rusted shut. She was efficient, never wasting a bit of rag or bone or chicken fat. Maybe because of Hank, she reminded me of a sewing machine, of the underside of a sewing machine, where it's all cogs and gears, not a flourish in sight, but a machine with a set task. The only thing she didn't do efficiently was die. The cancer that killed her was terrible, but it was not efficient. But all I said to Hank was yes, I remembered Eulalie Beecham. I glanced over at him, his hands that looked like bleached-out harlequin rags, his face gray, the skin around his eyes all loose with fatigue, though the eyes never wavered. All in all, his eyes gave you the sense of a bright blue flame atop a pale wax candle.

He motioned to the girl for more coffee and pushed his plate away without yet going after the pie. He rolled himself a cigarette. "I'll fire up New Year's Day 1917," he said with real pleasure, or maybe it was only pride and I couldn't tell the difference.

"Fire up what?"

"I can't tell you what, Doctor. I don't tell no one that. I never even told Martha. And Martha and me, we was close,

close as it's possible for a man and a woman to be. A woman like her, anyway. A man like me. But"—he seemed to shrug—"she wanted her divorce. Oh yes. And she was real worried I wouldn't give it to her. See, I set up just outside Douglas, Arizona Territory, oh, maybe a few days, a week afore she was to go to court. Oh, nothing too grand, but enough. Martha knows it, knows I'm there with my chemicals, working. And sure enough, the day for the divorce comes and there's big, black, sodden-looking clouds hunkered overhead." He smoked comfortably, and a little scrap of smile tugged at his lips.

"And?" I say. "And?"

"The judge knows who I am and what I do. He says to me, It's July, Mr. Beecham, and it don't usually rain in July in these parts. And I say, It don't usually rain in these parts a'tall, Your Honor."

"You were there? In the courtroom?" I ask, picturing the quivering, little, bird-brown Miss Emmons (that's the only way I could ever think of her, not as Mrs. Beecham at all; Mrs. Beecham was Eulalie), picturing tiny trembling Miss Emmons and the lanky Beecham and the black sky and the fearful judge.

"Oh, I was there. You think I was gonna let Martha just up and divorce me like it was nothing a'tall to me? I was there. It was my divorce too. Just like the wedding, that's how I reckoned it out. That's what I says to the judge when he says he hopes I haven't done nothing hasty which I will regret. I say: I regret this divorce, Your Honor. I regret my wife shedding me, leaving me, deserting me, Your Honor. I look over at Martha, hoping she would say something, but she don't. She sits real straight, staring at the judge like he's ordered her shot. So I go on and I tell the judge that a divorce day is like a wedding day. You don't get but one. Like a wedding, there oughta be something to mark such a day, something so's you won't forget it."

"Like rain in July?"

Hank's thin lips part, revealing yellowed teeth. "It didn't rain too much," he replied after a bit.

"And Miss Emmons?"

"You mean Martha? Oh, she got her divorce. The judge orders me to pay her money, a tidy sum too, but she said no, she didn't want my money and wouldn't take it neither. Didn't want nothing to do with me or my money or anything that smelled of sulphur or saltpeter or phosphorus or gunpowder. No smoke, says Martha to the judge, just like that, like the Declaration of Independence, she says it. She wanted only to be shut of me and have it forever final. Them's her words. Forever final. Martha could do words fine. And the judge says: Well, how will you live? And Martha says she'll go back to teaching, that she been a teacher afore she married me and she will be a teacher again. She said she had already got herself a job, up in some used-to-be town in the

Sierras, one of those places got its name and had its day in the gold rush. Paydirt, California." He drew phlegm up his nose. "Prob'ly no better than St. Elmo. Prob'ly worse," he added, applying himself to his pie.

I expected him to say something justifying, about how he felt equally happy to be shut of Miss Emmons, but he didn't. So I asked if there'd been any children.

"Everything might of been different if there would of been children. Martha always blamed it on me and my chemicals, said I'd blasted and fired up my insides all these years working with gunpowder and dynamite and phosphorous." He put his fork down. "I think Martha was too old. That's what I think. Even from the beginning." He put the cigarette between his lips but didn't light it. "I never said it, though. Not till I knew she was going to leave me. Not till I knew there was nothing I could do to keep her by my side. I said it then to give her pain." He shrugged. "I was going to lose her anyway."

"You must have loved her."

"Martha Emmons, she was a woman, all right," he said, nodding in secret agreement with himself. "Martha was always big on vows, vowing this and that, and so I told her, right there in the courtroom, I said, I vowed to love you, Martha, always, to cherish and protect. This judge, he can't change that vow. He can make us unmarried, but he can't change my loving you. Martha might of felt better for its being all clear and final with the law that she wasn't married to me no more, but it don't make no difference to me. I told her that when she left the court. I said, This divorce, it don't make no difference to me, Martha." He stretched out his arms and cracked his knuckles. "Martha says how I have broken her heart and she wishes I had a heart to break. Or something like that. She always had a way of talking so's you knew you'd been talked to, even if you wasn't quite sure what she said, even if she was dandered up and angry. It always was a pleasure to hear her give you a talk-to."

If she was still alive, I figured Miss Emmons was probably still cursing Hank Beecham (from some town that hung flapping on the side of a mountain, subsisting off lumber where it had once fattened on gold), cursing Hank Beecham from the squalid schoolhouse she believed she'd escaped forever when she ran off to marry him. "Did she love you?"

Something akin to surprise ruffled his features, and I thought perhaps I'd trod too close, infringed on his oxygen. He said (oddly, I thought) that Martha Emmons had loved him from the beginning to the end. That Martha had supported all his work and encouraged his study, his putting the grid of science over history. "Martha told me always to leave St. Elmo, to make something of myself, making rain. And that's what I did." His blasted eyebrows contracted in a frown. "And then she left me. Women are strange creatures."

"That they are."

"You ever marry, Doctor?"

"No. I might have once, but it's too late now."

"I told Martha, You knew what I was when you married me. I am what I am for your help and learning." He stretched out his legs and studied his thick boots. "Women aren't suited to a rainmaker's life, no more'n they are to battle. And when I make rain, it's like a battle, Doctor. And when I do battle, I'm always victorious. Victory's all that matters."

"Prometheus, you're his opposite. Prometheus stole fire from heaven. He stole it from the gods so men could warm themselves and cook and have light. You steal rain from nature, if not from the gods." I chuckled.

Hank did not laugh. "I steal rain from God." He struck a wooden match, a lucifer, on the bare table and seemed to inhale its strong phosphorous odor before he even lit his cigarette. "I battle God for rain. Victory's all that counts. Victory."

He went on after that, describing some of his most breathtaking victories, rain in Chihuahua, rain in Sonora, rain in Texas and Nevada, Arizona, places so dry St. Elmo looks swampy by contrast. He was careful to keep his discussion to the effects of his work and not the means of achieving those effects. And in truth, his telling of it did bring to mind battles. That was how he described his work, tactically, like a general, like Cleburne at Missionary Ridge, Chickamauga, Chattanooga, all those places where Cleburne had led and

Jeremiah Beecham had stubbornly, gallantly followed. He might once have been a brave man, Jeremiah, but what sorry specimen of a man beats his wife, thrashes his son, and rapes his daughter? Served Jeremiah Beecham right that the girl he misused stole his money and his one horse, and the boy he misused turned out to be one of those untutored geniuses, one of those people who there's no explanation for, who just come out of nowhere, just emerge bearing their talents like a mass of unshaped dough, asking the world: What shall I do with this? And then, whether the world tells them or not, they discover what to do with it. And they do it.

I finished my breakfast, smoked my cigar, listened to him give me a leisurely talk-to. He had used his talents, all right, made his rain and made it splendidly, but for a man in the business of damp, Hank Beecham was the driest creature alive. His bones rustled when he moved, like the legs of a cricket. He had a habit of rubbing his burned hands together, and of cracking his knuckles, as if the snap of his flesh might ignite all of its own. His eyes, though, they were Eulalie Beecham's, and I could hear her yet, *I'll never forget this, Doctor*, ringing in my ears, not like thanks but like a curse. Then I remind myself I am a man of science and don't believe in curses.

The depot was open, but we were in no real hurry. It was near nine when I took my leave from him. Hank insists on paying for breakfast and I thank him. He says, "I'll do better than buy you breakfast. I'll invite you out to the reservoir New Year's Day to witness what no man but me has ever seen. I'd be honored, Doctor. One man of science to another. You'll never forget this, Doctor. Never."

Of course, I said I'd be honored. And I was. I was pleased with myself that the rainmaker had invited me to see what he'd forbidden everyone else, and eager to announce that honor to Ruth and the family. I expected it might get me some admiration at Ruth's table during Sunday dinner, which I generally take with all of them. But even as Lil greeted me at the door at Ruth's big house on Silk Stocking Row, I knew that something was amiss. The very walls oozed tension. But no one will say what's amiss.

I join Ruth in the kitchen, where she's finishing up the apple-and-onion sauce for pork. I expect perhaps she'll tell me that Gideon, her eldest son, has had some setback or another since he's been living and working in Salt Lake with

Ruth's miserly brother. But no, Gideon's fine, she says, going grimly about her work. And I admit I wouldn't have been stunned to hear something unsavory about Mason, Ruth's other son. Mason is as surly, sluggish, and crafty now at eighteen as he was at eight and will likely be at eighty, so I would have been prepared for some foolery from Mason. But no.

So, everything ready, I follow Ruth into the dining room and take my place at the opposite end of the table from her, and I look down the table at the family assembled: Mason, Afton, Tom Lance (Afton's husband), Lil (just twenty-one and a widow already, poor lovely Lil). I say, "Where's Cissa?" She is the youngest of Ruth's tribe.

"She'll be here presently," says Ruth sharply.

As if on cue, Cissa sidles round the dining-room door and takes her place beside me, her head hung low and her hair bobbed off at the ears. My breath comes in a *whoosh* because nothing could have prepared me for this: the sight of Cissa Douglass (sixteen years old and a good Mormon girl) with the only bare female neck in this town, saving for a couple of truly desperate girls doing the best they can to make a living at the St. Elmo Pleasure Palace. I do not mention them. I am speechless. I say so. "Cissa, I'm speechless."

"Well, that's good," Cissa snaps. "I've heard enough talk about chickens to last me my whole life."

"Chickens?" I query down the table at the faces assembled there. "Where?"

Ruth gives me the look women reserve for the truly mis-guided men in their lives. She says crisp words to the effect that Cissa's reference to chickens reflects the family's unani-mous disgust with her bobbed hair, an outrage she (Cissa) had perpetrated Friday at Bowers' Barber Shop, and that *ev-eryone* who has seen Cissa agrees she looks like a plucked chicken.

I do not dispute Ruth's claim to correctness (yet I chuckle to myself, because I told Ruth a long time ago that though Cissa did not have Lil's beauty nor Afton's starch, still Cissa would be more of a trial to her than those girls combined). But I am moved to take Cissa's part in the situation. Maybe it's the sight of her neck, so vulnerable, or maybe it's just my nature to take up unpopular causes. "I believe I like your hair bobbed short, Cissa," I say, pleased to see the hangdog look depart from her eyes. "I think I do like it. It sets off your cheekbones." I look at all the rest of the family, even Ruth, and go on to defend Cissa. "There's no law says women must have long hair and men short. Short hair is sensible and healthful, and more women should do it. Yes," I add, warm-ing to the subject, "maybe the time has come for bobbed hair and votes for women."

Cissa takes up the refrain. "There is a New Woman. The New Woman of the twentieth century will not be the slave of men, or throw away her rights or freedom just because men say she doesn't need them. She will not let men vote for her or speak for her."

"I never heard anything so foolish!" Afton looks to her husband for support, but Tom says nothing.

Mason snickers, "Cissa's a suffragist. She wants to vote and smoke. Wear pants, maybe."

"Women will get the vote," Cissa maintains. And then, with a look to me (I nod in accordance with women getting the vote), she picks up speed and goes on, declaring herself on the side of progress and the twentieth century, and how the old ideas and the nineteenth century have been completely discredited, are being blown to bits on the battlefields of France right now. Having been born in 1900 (she finishes up), she intends to be a woman of the twentieth century and not a slave to the past.

"Who told you all this nonsense?" asks Ruth.

"No one had to tell me. It's in the air. There is a new age coming."

Give that girl credit for audacity, I think, suppressing a chuckle.

Mason says, "What good will it be to be a New Woman, if it's just the same old men?"

"If women change," I observe, "men will have to."

Cissa gives me a look of triumphant gratitude and a smile. Cissa can work that smile on any man. I am not immune. With that smile, I am her ally against all of them, Ruth too, if need be. I brought Narcissa Douglass into this world, the youngest of six children. It was a difficult birth, and Ruth was a difficult woman, but unique and fascinating, and we have been to one another open friends and secret lovers, neither of which her religion would allow her and all St. Elmo would condemn.

Ruth asks Mason to give the blessing, which I sit through, tolerate, though I am no believer (and if I was, I still wouldn't be a Mormon). The family tolerates my not believing, and they don't oblige me to subscribe to superstition and humbug. Prayers mercifully past, the fried potatoes, the fried squash (boiling would use a gallon jug), the porkchops with the apple-and-onion sauce go round the table, and I take the opportunity to deflect attention from Cissa's neck and announce that I have been invited by the rainmaker, Hank Beecham himself, "to watch him fire up on New Year's Day, one man of science to another."

"Fire up what?" says Ruth.

"Well, that I don't know. That's his secret. I get to be a witness, that's all. He's going to make rain."

"Only God can make rain," declares Afton. Afton Lance's ideas might come from the Mormons, but her certitude regarding the Almighty is all her very own.

"Well," I say, passing round the potatoes, "to his credit, Hank Beecham makes no claim to be God. He's a man of science. He learned to put the grid of science over history."

To this, Afton launches into a soliloquy worthy of Bishop

Lew Cannon himself, about how the city never should have hired Hank in the first place, how if St. Elmo wanted rain, they should pray harder. Ruth makes no comment. Neither religion, politics, nor science holds any allure for Ruth Douglass. I know her better than anyone on this earth, and the word *if* just will not form on her lips. Afton's Tom, he says nothing because he's not a talker (good thing, since Afton talks for the two of them). Mason's mouth is full. His mouth is always full. And Lil, always happiest in Afton's shadow, nods in complete agreement with her older sister as Afton holds the floor with her talk of rain and drought and Hank Beecham's work being contrary to God's will. But I am surprised when Afton finishes and Cissa pipes up, announcing she'd like to go.

"Go where?" Ruth asks.

"With Doctor. Wherever it is he's going to watch Mr. Beecham fire up on New Year's Day." Cissa rubs her bare neck and goes on. "I am interested in science and progress. Science and progress will dominate the twentieth century. I want to be a witness to this great event."

Afton snorts. (Afton Lance has a snort that is going to be absolutely intolerable in another ten years.) And because Afton snorts, Lil sniffs. Mason gives out a bellicose *Ha ha ha* till Ruth gives him the eye, and then he shuts up.

In the interest of science, progress, and the twentieth century (which I have just championed), I have to say, "I would encourage young people—girls and boys—to be interested in science. I'd say to any young lady that she *ought* to be interested in the world around her. Yes, she should. If you'd like to come, Cissa, well, you're welcome. If it's all right with you, Ruth," I add quickly.

Ruth gives Cissa a look that says, *What are you up to?* But she agrees that Cissa can go.

Cissa tilts her chin and smiles at all of us. "One day, I'll be able to tell my grandchildren I saw science in the flesh. Ain't that right, Doctor?"

"*Isn't,*" says Ruth. "And I don't think we need to talk about the flesh at the table. Isn't that right, Lucius?"

"Yes," I say, "that's right."

CHAPTER EIGHT

arcissa Douglass didn't give a hang for science. But she had put herself so squarely on the side of science and progress that when New Year's Day came and Doctor Tipton called for her that morning—so early it was scarcely light—she was ready. At least Doctor treated her like a grown lady and did not care what she'd done to her hair, nor did he question her right to do it. Narcissa made conversation befitting a New Woman as they drove down Silk Stocking Row. She wished it was bright daylight so everyone on Silk Stocking Row could watch Miss Narcissa Douglass riding in the Flyer in her twill jumper, her coat with velvet cuffs, her patent leather shoes, white stockings, and smart new hat. She wished she was wearing a silk crepe blouse instead of cotton, pretended she was. Since she was at it, why not further imagine Miss Narcissa Douglass in a tailored traveling suit, periwinkle in color, with a long automobile coat, fine-grained gray leather gloves, and a hat especially for the outing, a toque, say, with a neat little motoring veil?

It was a cold dry morning with a razor-sharp wind as they passed through town heading east and upward into the foothills. St. Elmo, never a city addicted to aesthetic niceties, was even less impressive in the drought. Yards and shrubs were brown as the back of an old dog, and palm trees hung their heads, shabby as dirty brooms. Beyond the town, tumbleweeds clung to rickety fences or broke free and blew before the Flyer. Doctor remarked that they all looked like waltzing beggars.

Cissa blinked twice, but they still looked like tumbleweeds to her.

"I am proud to have you along, Cissa. I do believe we're going to see something up here that no one else has ever witnessed. I think we're going to see science taming the weather, harnessing it for the good of mankind, a real instance of progress and man's ability to know and control the elements."

"I am proud to be here, Doctor," she replied. "Proud to see what's been forbidden the rest of the world. Science in the flesh," she repeated, freed of her mother's objections.

Lucius paused and frowned. "I hope Hank won't mind my bringing you up with me."

Cissa rubbed her bare neck reflectively. "It'll be so nice to have rain. Imagine trying to take a bath *and* wash your hair with just a gallon jug! It's impossible. It's revolting," she added with relish.

"And a good reason to bob your hair off altogether," observed Lucius.

She gave him a conspirator's smile, a smile more inspired than anything she could have said.

The Flyer ground and grumbled up the road, which grew rougher as it rose, just a sort of rugged thread climbing, twisting around the mountain. The Army Corps of Engineers had made this road, and the county maintained it, touting its possibilities for vistas, though all you could see was St. Elmo itself, and once the track went into the hills, climbed toward the reservoir, you could not even see that. The mountains closed in behind you, the road became narrow and steep, the inclines treacherous, and any sense of vista was lost. As they wound up into the hills, they saw thin branches of black smoke wafting into the clear, hard, cloudless sky.

The Urquita Reservoir sat in a high wide saddle of land, the Army Corps of Engineers' road skirting it, a fringe of woods and brush beyond the road. It was dry now, holding only dust, leaves, and debris. The broad reservoir bed was cracked open, seamed as an old earthenware bowl. Rabbitbrush,

sagebrush, rocks, stubborn piñon pines, junipers, and leaf-
less thickets clustered here and there. Cissa and Doctor were
high enough that it was a good deal colder than down in
the valley. They followed the road and came in sight of a
rise directly behind the reservoir, a cleared plain, probably
once the bivouac of the engineers, surrounded by the same
mongrel woods. And here, before the brush and pines and
junipers, they were greeted by the strangest sight ever in St.
Elmo County.

The Flyer idled noisily while they stared. Four steel windmill towers fifty feet high, supporting at their tops not windmills but four vats—copper wash boilers—on four broad
metal trays. These were set in a wide half-circle. Some little
distance away and in an opposing arc were four huge iron
cauldrons—big as cook pots for the gods—and from these
the acrid black smoke wafted. Cissa and Doctor could hear
the snap of wood burning beneath these cauldrons. Lucius
stared out over the plain. "It reminds me of something from
my school days, Cissa," he said, "like a picture I might once
have seen in reading *The Iliad* as a boy, the battle set up to
appease Achilles' wrath."

Cissa's education in the St. Elmo city schools was classi-
cally lapsed, but she knew her Bible. She asked if Mr.
Beecham intended to feed the five hundred from these pots.

"In a manner of speaking, Cissa. If he can bring rain, it
will amount to the same thing. And not just for us here in

California. The war in Europe has ruined their crops, and they are in dire need of food and forage for their animals. Europe will be starving soon if we can't supply them."

The steel towers dwarfed the Flyer, and as they trundled past the huge cook pots, the Flyer audibly evinced mechanical distrust. They stopped and alighted not far from two windowless tin tents. Clearly, one shack had been for the Chinese, who had since departed, and the other was for Hank Beecham. A thin vein of woodsmoke came from a tin pipe in the roof. A path had been cleared—raked, if not graded—and the stones pulled up and tossed aside. A few dead birds, victims of the smoke, lay here and there as though in state, their bodies undisturbed. A wagon stood before the tin shacks, its shafts useless on the ground, its hand brake set. The heavy hardworking horse Hank had bought was saddled, bridled, ready to ride, but tied incongruously to the back of the wagon. The horse looked up quickly at their approach, its eyes wide, nervous, and expectant, and it whinnied and stamped. Doctor called out Hank's name, and a tin door swung open on crude hinges. There stood Hank Beecham, shocked to see Cissa. He frowned and said he'd told Doctor to come alone.

Lucius colored. "This is Miss Narcissa Douglass, a young friend of mine and a person very much interested in science and history. A student of science and history."

Cissa said, "Pleased to meet you," and waited for Mr.

Beecham to say something polite, but he screwed his eyes at her. They were hard eyes, empty as the sky overhead. He was tall, without much hair, and what he had was grizzled, and his hands were horrible to behold. Cissa could not take her eyes from those hands. The skin, all different colors, was pale and puckered. "Science and history are my favorite pursuits," she added weakly.

"I have nothing for schoolgirls here." Hank Beecham's pants were stuffed into rubber boots, and he had little notes pinned up and down his suspenders. Despite the January morning, he was not wearing a coat nor even a shirt, just faded red underwear.

"Cissa's not asking for anything special, Hank. She wants to tell her grandchildren she's seen science making rain. She's here as a witness for the future. For the twentieth century."

Hank growled and fumed, and Cissa winced slightly from the downwind sniff of him. He was charred and singed and hairless as the proverbial pullet about to get the skewer and the spit. If this was science in the flesh, Cissa could do without it, but she could not say so now.

Without another word, Hank beckoned them into the tin shed and dusted off a powder keg, nodded to Cissa, ordered her to sit there. Reluctantly, she did. The floor was dirt and the stench suffocating. It reminded Cissa of one of their rented houses in St. Elmo, which had been infested with lice and fleas and rats, and before they moved in, her mother had set up charcoal braziers and burned brimstone, observing acidly that if the house exploded, it would be a mercy to the vermin. Cissa glanced over to the tiny firebox—too small to be called a stove—and there, right beside a homely coffeepot, was brimstone burning, and the smell choked her nose and made her eyes run. The shack was lit by a brace of candles set upon a tin dish, the flames so densely blue they scarcely illuminated anything. Beside the firebox was a camp bed and beneath it pairs of rubber boots, piles of rags, and Hank's satchel. From her perch on the powder keg, Cissa saw that powder kegs also supported planking that passed for a table, which was neatly laid out with a strange array of goods, a banquet for the devil, thought Cissa, whose Mormon faith had formed her frame of reference. There were vials and boxes and jars, some with cork stoppers and some with glass. Corks of uniform size were lined up like regiments before stacks of white paper folded in tentlike caps. Cissa stared at them.

"I make my own rockets," Hank explained curtly.

Cissa nodded. At the most distant reach of the table, as far away as possible from the candles, a yellow waxy substance glowed luminously in the near-dark. Beneath the table were jugs and buckets, pails, copper cookers, and a twenty-five-pound scale, its weights all lined up neatly. Every time anyone moved, the air inside the tin shack ruffled with the smell of linseed oil, pitch, camphor gum, and resin. Minute measuring spoons, cups, and ladles were hung on hooks, and an assortment of pokers and long wooden spatulas, long-handled tin paddles, and hollow glass tubes were laid out like cutlery. Everything was arranged neatly, as if guests were about to arrive.

Lucius too was pale from the burning brimstone smell. He drew out a handkerchief and mopped his face, remarking awkwardly to Cissa, "In science, precision is everything."

"You got to have instincts first," Hank contradicted. "Precision, you can come by that with trial and error. Instinct's different."

Hank poured some coffee for himself and Doctor into tin cups, offered one to Cissa, who declined. She would have liked to accept, but she had been raised a good Mormon—though she did not have the instincts of one.

"Your clothes won't do," said Hank, grumbling again about how he hadn't expected no children, and giving Lucius a hard look. Cissa was further alarmed when he added that the way she was dressed, she'd go home looking like a singed pullet. The chicken imagery angered her—and besides, she'd thought the pullet better described him. He dug beneath the camp bed and took out a man's flannel shirt and a cheap brown workingman's coat with rivets and flaps. He took two pairs of motoring goggles off a hook and handed them to Lucius and Cissa. "You both do everything just like I tell you."

Hank took a huge red bandanna, faded and old, and told Cissa to take off her hat and cover her hair with it. She obeyed, and he looked shocked to see her hair bobbed, but he said nothing, only pointed to pairs of rubber boots under the camp bed. He told them both to put on a pair. "There's small ones should fit you," he said with a curt nod to Cissa. "I had to buy them for the Chinks. Doctor, you'd best take the Flyer a mile or so back down the road and leave it near the dam. You don't know what will happen with this much powder. This is more powder than . . ." He drank his coffee without another word.

Doctor put on his rubber boots, finished his coffee, and tramped outside. They heard the Flyer cough and start. Hank busied himself, his back to Cissa, his sole remark being that he would need the keg she was sitting on.

Cissa got up, pulled off her lovely Sunday shoes, and stuck her white-stockinged feet into men's nasty rubber boots last worn by some heathen Chinese. She wondered if she could change her mind, go home, but something about Hank Beecham made her afraid to ask. Something about his hands and the way he smelled. The way the whole airless place smelled. She did gather enough courage, however, to ask if she could wait outside. Hank grunted in assent, advising her in no uncertain terms to stay beside the horse and wagon, not to venture into the other shack nor up toward the towers. "I'm sure I won't be tempted," Cissa replied, making her exit. She gulped great drafts of air once she was safely outside.

She was certainly glad that the boys at St. Elmo High could not see her now. The boots, the shirt, the rough coat that hung down beyond her hands, the goggles pulled over her eyes, and the red bandanna over her head, Cissa did not feel like a lady anymore, and certainly not a New Woman. She was a lone girl standing by a wagon and a huge, ugly, unkempt horse that snorted, yanked on his bridle, and kicked, eager to escape her. Cissa was eager to escape him too. She went around to the front of the wagon, sat on the shafts, and kicked dead spiders in the dirt till Doctor returned, puffing from the exertion. She brightened her expression on his account, and he responded, his mobile mouth curling into a smile. "It's like watching Vulcan, isn't it, Cissa?"

"Who?"

"Vulcan, the god of fire, who forged Jove's thunderbolts and Achilles' armor."

"I don't believe I know them, Doctor, but if you mean it stinks around here, I'd agree to that."

Hank came out and pointed them to a group of boulders some quarter-mile distant in the direction of the reservoir. "You'll be safer there," said Hank, handing Lucius two pairs of field glasses, "but you can still see everything. Science wedded to history. You'll never forget this, Doctor."

From the boulders, standing up and peering over their protection, Cissa and Doctor used the field glasses to watch Hank Beecham in front of his shed. He unpinned one of the papers from his suspenders, gave it a quick read, and stuffed it in his pocket. He went inside the shed where the Chinese had slept and brought out, one after another, half a dozen kegs of powder and several boxes of dynamite. "I pity the Chinese, trying to sleep in there," murmured Doctor. "Their dreams must have been unsettling."

They watched as Hank untied the horse from the wagon, looping its reins, loosely tied to a nearby stake. He then loaded the powder and dynamite in the back of the wagon, walked around to the front, grabbed hold of the shafts, and, like a beast of burden himself, pulled the wagon, walking slowly, gingerly, tapping the way before him as though he were blind, kicking any rocks from his path as he made his way toward the tall steel towers and their opposing cauldrons.

"What's he doing?" asked Cissa.

"Making sure he don't get blown to bits. I hope I haven't . . ." But Doctor gulped and did not finish.

Hank stopped at a point equidistant between the cauldrons and the steel windmill towers. He walked to the most distant cauldron, hunkered down in front of the fire, and stabbed at it with a long poker. With the field glasses, they watched him rise, lean closer to the pot, and sniff into its sulphurous emission. When he turned around, his face was black with whatever foul soot was drifting lazily up, but he seemed satisfied.

"I think he's cooking missionaries in there. That's what I think," Cissa observed. "I'm sure that's just what a cannibal looks like when he's got his missionary in the pot. My Sunday school teacher told us what the heathens do, how they cook up missionaries like you would a turnip."

"Oh, Cissa, he's cooking something, but not missionaries. I don't know what it is, but there's something here I hadn't reckoned on. Something ugly."

Cissa put her field glasses down. "I think he's a Son of Perdition, Doctor. You know, like the Church teaches us, the Sons of Perdition are the worst sinners, people who God has truly turned His face from because they're so wicked and lost and beyond redemption. The Sons of Perdition, they go where the fires never stop, Doctor, and it's not just for their sins and wickedness. It's because there's no remorse."

Lucius preferred not to comment on Mormon doctrine. He was more interested in watching Hank hit the bung on one of the powder kegs and carefully walk round and round the cauldron, perhaps four feet from the flames, spilling black powder in a fine even line, making a sort of black target with the cauldron as the bull's-eye. Then he opened a box of dynamite and placed twelve sticks—arranged as neatly as Roman numerals on a sundial—outside the black circle, their fuses pointing in toward the pots. He repeated this process on the second cauldron and then, at a smart pace, pulled the wagon back to the house and loaded up again.

"I have to pee," said Cissa, not even bothering to be a New Woman.

"Well, go on over there behind those rocks and be quick about it."

"Why should I? He's taking forever."

"I told you be quick about it," Doctor snapped.

"Oh, I wish I'd never come. I'm cold and hungry, and if this is science, it's just dull. I always knew history was dull, but this is worse."

"This is worse," Doctor returned, his throat dry, his words parched, apprehension knotting his brows as he watched Hank perform without haste or grandeur these same rituals around the other two cauldrons, his movements measured, precise, rehearsed. Once finished, he pulled the wagon away from the semicircle, and giving it one massive heave—Lucius was surprised at his strength—Hank thrust it toward the surrounding brush. Hank dusted his hands and stepped with a new alacrity toward a keg of gunpowder standing alone and awaiting orders. Lucius's field glasses told him there was a look of peculiar pleasure on Hank's blackened face, not a smile but some inarticulate particular pleasure. Hank held the small keg under one arm and dribbled out a trail from each cauldron toward a central point nearer the sheds. When

Lucius pulled the field glasses from his eyes and surveyed the whole, he saw that Hank had created the ribs of a gunpowder fan. A gunpowder fan and dynamite bull's-eyes. "I'll be damned," Lucius whispered. "I'll be damned. I never believed . . ."

"Why is he walking like that?" Cissa asked Doctor as, avoiding the ribs of the fan, Hank stepped gingerly toward the towers.

"Like what?"

"Like he's got dynamite in his pants."

"Oh, Cissa, that man can't walk any other way. Oh, Cissa, I'm a fool! I never should have let you come."

"It's all right, Doctor." Cissa patted his immaculate, well-known hand. "I wanted to come. I'm interested. Really."

Lucius put the field glasses back to his eyes and saw that, on each tower, a long and tangled skein of wires—braided or at least gathered together and secured with a rope—had been tied near the ground to an iron anchor post. The knots of wires looked to be as thick as a man's wrist. Lucius took the field glasses slowly up the towers to the top, to the tubs. For the first time, he noted the iron rings around the outer rim, each ring holding a rocket; inside, similar rings held rockets in place. The washtubs were brimming over not with clean white wash, but with the clean white caps of rockets. Pendent from the trays which held this explosive laundry, suspended like the bodies of troublesome possums, were aerial shells. He saw that the loose lines tied to the anchor posts were actually long intermingling fuses, patiently gathered together as a woman might gather the threads of a blanket she was knitting, as a man might gather the reins of a team of workhorses. It took his breath away. Reaching in, up under his ribs, apprehension squeezed at his liver till the taste of bile overwhelmed him and he knew that for all his education, his experience, his intelligence, the range of his scientific inquiries, he was ignorant of what was about to befall him. Dumb before the events that were about to unfold.

In these cauldrons, these fires, Lucius suddenly recollected himself as a boy playing with wooden soldiers before the fireplace at his grandmother's house. Women's voices and laughter wafted from another room. Then—*thump, thump*—he heard the horrible progress of the one-legged uncle, the veteran of Shiloh, coming closer and closer. The uncle stopped before the child and the fireplace and the toy soldiers. The boy's gaze lifted fearfully to his face. With a grin and a grunt, the uncle swooped down, snatched up a handful of toy soldiers, broke their wooden legs off in a single sharp snap, and threw the whole into the fire. The boy instinctively reached toward the fire to save the toy soldiers, burned his hands, and the uncle leaned down, whispering in his carbolic breath, *It rained legs that day, rained legs and arms. That day, it rained fire.* And suddenly, Lucius knew what was going to happen here. Not why. Only what. Instinctively as the child Lucius had reached into the fire to save the soldiers, Doctor stood upright, fled the shelter of the boulders, and ran, arms waving up and down, yelling out for Hank to stop, ran toward the gunpowder ribs that converged where Hank stood with the ropes, the reins, the fuses from all four towers looped over one arm.

Hank's eyes narrowed to watch Lucius running, arms waving, through the smoky ribbons which blew from the cauldrons. He ignored Doctor's cry to stop, busying himself briefly with the fuses. Then he took out his papers and tobacco.

"Hank!" Lucius called breathlessly, once abreast of him. "You have to stop."

Rolling himself a cigarette, his fingers absolutely steady, Hank said, "I told you how it is. Every rainstorm, every one is different, but the feeling is the same. There's a glory in it." His thin lips splintered briefly, his craggy hairless face suffused with satisfaction. "There's victory."

"Who are you fighting? *Four* towers? *Four* cauldrons? God knows what else you've—"

"God's got nothing to do with it."

"It's St. Elmo, isn't it? You've set up a hell here especially for St. Elmo. You don't want rain, you want—"

"Fifty thousand dollars says I can fill that reservoir. I'm good at what I do."

"Don't go through with this, Hank, I beg of you."

Hank scrutinized him levelly as he lit his cigarette, the wooden match seeming to ignite spontaneously in the sulphurous air. "I'm about to give this humpbacked town rain. I don't mean some little drizzle-piss puddle, I mean real rain. Rain like they had at Shiloh, Doctor. At Chickamauga and Waterloo, at Austerlitz—and the Somme, Doctor, rain like they got over in Europe right now."

"That's war, Hank! In Europe, right now, that's war! Do you want war?"

"I want victory."

"Hank—"

"You're under orders. I'm the general here. Get back to that boulder. There'll be no harm come to you and that girl as long as you obey my orders."

At the mention of Cissa, Lucius faltered, as though he had just remembered her. He looked toward the boulders to see her small, goggle-clad face peering over.

Squatting low, reaching out, Hank lit the center, the fan, the gunpowder ribs. The flames hissed, quarreled briefly with the earth on which they had been laid, but finally flared, sparkled blue and white, and Hank stood up, watching them rip and rattle. "Go, sir. You got time to get to the boulders if you run like hell now." The flames chased each other along the ground and up the lines of gunpowder.

So Lucius ran. He heard but did not see Hank cry,

"Attack, you sonsofbitches!" He did not see the dancing flames frolic toward the cauldrons, heard but did not see Hank whoop, an ear-piercing yell that spooked the horse, which kicked and gnashed and tore its reins loose from the stake and, once freed, galloped headlong toward Hank. Lucius did not see Hank, cigarette still dangling from his lips, swear viciously at the animal tearing amongst the cauldrons. Lucius, running, his eyes on Cissa, heard a cry, raw and raucous, Hank goddamning the horse. His back to the rainmaker and the wild-eyed horse streaking through the neatly laid gunpowder fans, Lucius did not see Hank try to use the glowing nub of his cigarette to light the knot of fuses, which did not, would not, ignite. Hank put the cigarette back between his lips and, squinting against the smoke, drew from his pocket a matchbox and a fistful of wooden matches, the well-named lucifers. These he struck only once before he held aloft a blaze that would have singed a man not already far beyond that poor pain. He lit the four fuse cords one by one, without haste or anxiety, his hands seemingly aflame. Doctor did not see Hank Beecham standing there at the center of all he had created and was about to create, about to unleash, watching the flames snake their way out to the cauldrons, lit fuses sparkling up the tall, tall towers to the washtubs full of rockets and the trays holding aerial shells, the all-hell he was about to break loose.

Doctor did not see this because, once back at the boulders, he and Cissa, goggles and all, looked at one another like people with much to say and no time to say it. Cissa dove down and Doctor did too, his arms over her back, his whole body protectively bent over her, crouching down and holding her, pressing both of them against the earth just before the four explosions sounded from under the cauldrons, a heartbeat separating them.

The ground gave way. They were knocked flat, Lucius sprawled over Cissa, the boulders around them rumbling, trembling, breaking free from their accustomed sockets in the earth, rocks flying, hitting their bodies, clods flying like missiles, dirt and smoke swirling everywhere, choking them so they could not breathe. Pelted with debris and the blasted bodies of small animals, sundered squirrels, rabbits, they felt the earth groan and bellow, Doctor holding Cissa as she screamed that they were going to die, that God was going to kill them, whatever else she said or might have said completely drowned under another quartet of explosions, the four towers, only one of which came down, the other three standing, belching up their fiery protest, the rockets shooting, piercing the blue to make it bleed fire, fiery arrows to draw rain from the inimical sky. Shells whinnied, screeched, sang their high explosive arias, and burst overhead. It rained fire.

Lucius Tipton saw this. Keeping Cissa pressed down, he looked up, tilted his head back, and beheld fire-streaking crescendos filling the sky, flame fountains, saw the fusillade of flares igniting overhead, shells bursting like miscreant stars, man-made meteors flinging themselves against the enemy, leaving long ripples of smoke to saunter down. Even through the thick black smoke, these things were visible, as though night had fallen and day must be rekindled. Great booms rumbled beneath them and overhead. This was not merely Vulcan's forge, but Vulcan's military band, all the gods enlisted, all playing fire. This was war.

Then he turned and suddenly beheld Hank Beecham, who had once again gathered his mortal molecules there beside Lucius, crouching behind the boulders, only this time, he was blackened and soot stained, and smoke trailed visibly off his body, and he stank of singed hair and flesh.

Cissa thought she had died, been cremated, and gone to hell all in the same moment. As Cissa rose slowly out of her crouch, she shrieked to see on Doctor's shoulder a grisly clump of flesh. She screamed again and again, thinking he'd been wounded, but Lucius brushed the bloody glob from his shoulder. Then he brushed from the red bandanna on her head another bloody glob, this one with hair, not hers, but Cissa screeched and gibbered and wept just the same, and Lucius could not comfort her.

Hank Beecham cursed the goddamn horse. Then his black lips parted to reveal yellow teeth. "Victory. What did I tell you?" Another explosion rattled the very earth beneath them, the very air they breathed. "I told you, you'd never forget this!"

Another shower of earth and rock hit them, another explosion blasted the air and sky, more shells and rockets screamed their impossible sopranos, then flew apart and left the sky singed with their honor.

Damn me all to hell. Damn me for ever taking that girl, for putting Cissa in danger. Damn me for thinking it would be fancy fireworks, rockets' red glare, Fourth of July, for not guessing it would be the Western Front come to St. Elmo County. Damn me for thinking that Hank Beecham gave a good goddamn for science or history either. Hank cared only for the fire and destruction he brought down, the blast and battle he'd joined against the God he claimed he didn't believe in. He was fighting God. On God's turf and God's terms. He wanted only victory.

I pulled Cissa up close to me so I could see her eyes through the motoring goggles, through the darkness that had descended on the earth between the bursts that lit up the sky. I told her, "Just do everything I say, Cissa, just follow my orders," though I did not know what those orders would be, save for retreat. Somehow, I had to get us out of there. I said not another word to Hank Beecham, who, like a general, watched the war he'd unleashed between science and history, the brimstone battle. Field glasses in hand, Hank peered over the boulders. I took Cissa's hand. Trench-bound soldiers fleeing No Man's Land, we bent double and made our way as best we could toward the reservoir. And even bent double, we sometimes couldn't breathe or see, and we were reduced to all fours, crawling, crawling.

The explosions continued, the ground rumbling, the sky bursting into bouquets of fire, twisted stems of smoke. I blessed whatever presence of mind or forethought I'd had in paying attention to such small landmarks as there were across the reservoir. There were damn few anyway, and they were obscured, altered almost beyond recognition in the pall. I had only small faith in my sense of direction and the hope that it wasn't my time to die. At least not like this. Not with Cissa needing me. I blessed God I'd left the Flyer down by the dam at all, a mile or so away, because without it, I'd be stuck in these infernal mountains with a sixteen-year-old girl my solemn responsibility and no way down. If anything happened to Cissa—well, I willed myself deaf to such thoughts, and deaf to such thoughts as whispered maybe the Flyer hadn't survived the blasts. Willed myself and Cissa to that reservoir and then across it, toward the dam and the Flyer.

A foul wind now took its foul cue and blew after us, over us, pressed and oppressed us as we crossed the hard-caked reservoir floor while the phosphorous fires from the towers burned and the rockets went off and the cauldrons cooked their lethal brew, spewing it into the air. Me and Cissa, never quite upright but running when we could and crawling when we couldn't, we crossed that long mile over the reservoir, joining every jackrabbit and ground squirrel, gopher, snake, and coyote whose flesh hadn't been blown to bits (and crawling around the bodies of those that had), till I see the road though I'd missed the dam, veered off course in the smoke and confusion, but I blessed the road, and I could hear, behind us, trees falling, snapping, burning. The woods surrounding the plain had caught fire too. With this wind, no telling where it would burn to. To hell, I reckoned, and I cursed Hank Beecham again.

I scrambled out of the reservoir, pulling Cissa behind me, our clothes in tatters, our legs and hands badly bloodied. I followed the road, figuring that even if I'd missed the direct route to the dam, I could find the Flyer via the road. And I did. Still standing, tires intact, smothered in dirt and debris, dented with the force of flying rocks, windshield cracked and opaque as ice. I took the crank out of the toolbox and smashed out the windshield, making Cissa stand back some distance till it shattered, and then with a single sweep, I brushed the glass away. And from the toolbox too, I took the blanket I always carry and the canteens of water. I wrapped Cissa in the blanket, thrust the canteens in her arms, and told her to get in. Then I went round and cranked the old Flyer, praying (yes, me praying) that it would not fail me now, praying and blessing and damning the Flyer and myself all in the same breath, cranking like all hell till at last I hear the old chug and chortle of the engine. It was enough to make a Baptist of me.

The explosions still rattling the ground beneath us, we make our way down an inch at a time, using my wits to navigate, needing a sextant because the smoke is thicker than any fog at sea and the way perilous, the road falling off into steep ravines. It was a narrow track in the best of times, and in the smoke and fading light, I only hoped I could keep us on the road, ease us down. The brakes on the Flyer started to burn, and that smell joined with the black smoke trailing down after us, even down the foothills as we came in sight of St. Elmo, which was stewing under a dark-colored cloud that seemed the size of Africa.

The smoke and stench had singed my hair and burnt my lungs and sucked the oxygen from my blood. I didn't dare take the goggles off till I'd almost come out of the hills altogether. Even then, the feeble lamps of the Flyer lit up the grit and cinder, the ash and smoke everywhere.

We'd come to the outskirts of town, where the streets draggle into the desert. I reached over and touched Cissa's shoulder, patted it. She was still all wrapped up in the blanket, stone silent. I could feel her trembling. I tried to speak, to say something, anything, but my lips were pasted shut with soot, smoke coats my tongue and throat and lungs. Finally, I get out a few curses, damning myself again and again. I feel her little shoulders heaving. "Forgive me, Cissa. I didn't know. I never guessed. I was a fool. You were a real brave girl up there, Cissa. It's over now." Looking skyward, not believing it was over but saying it just the same, I bring my eyes back to the road before me, my hands to the wheel.

The blanket falls back from her head, and slowly Cissa turns her face to mine. Her face is entirely filthy and her lips are bruised and bloody. Her eyes are empty of everything save for tears and fears. I reach over and pull the goggles down from her eyes and she starts to cry, to bawl, wiping her face and nose in long swipes with her bleeding hands. I long to put my arms around her but dare not stop. I tell her again how brave she is. How brave she has been. I motion to her to drink from the canteen and she does and it seems to help. She takes several swills, three or four, because the first few she spits out. She hands me the canteen and I do likewise. I say again, "Damn me, Cissa. Forgive me. I had no idea. I never guessed."

"Don't worry about me, Doctor. Worry about Mother,"

Cissa says, after collecting herself. She sits up straight, pulling the blanket round her shoulders like it was the flag. Give that girl credit for audacity. By heaven, if there is a New Woman, Narcissa Douglass is it.

Once we come into St. Elmo proper, Cissa pulls Hank's red bandanna off her hair and wipes her face with it, and I am shocked to see her short bright hair is still golden, the only thing shining for miles. People are coming out of their houses, standing on the streets, the women with hankies over their mouths, the men in shirtsleeves, all of them looking to the east. I have a glance over my shoulder, and in the sky, you could still see blasts and bursts of light in high arcs above the mountains, flares streaking up and bursting. The sky soaked up the smoke the way gauze soaks up blood.

As I turn up Silk Stocking Row, Art Whickham himself flags me down, leaps in front of the Flyer with his arms waving, screaming at me. Art hangs on the Flyer, pounding, demanding to know what in hell happened up there, what in hell Beecham is doing. I bring the Flyer to a choking halt.

Cissa says, "Excuse me, Uncle Art," opens the door, leans out, and vomits at his feet, then wipes her lips with the red bandanna. "It was quite something, Uncle Art," she says coolly. "I would not have missed it for the world."

"Beecham's going to blow us all to kingdom come!" shrieks Art, ignoring Cissa. "What's he doing up there? What's he—"

"He's making war, Whickham. He's making the war you bought and may still have to pay for. Caveat emptor, Whickham! Let the buyer beware! Now get the hell out of my way, or by God I'll mow you down where you stand!" I pull the Flyer past him and leave him in the street.

Ruth starts running down Silk Stocking Row soon as she sees the Flyer coming. Lil and Mason are out front like everyone else, coughing from the chemical stench and watching smoke turn the sky blacker yet. Ruth flings herself upon the Flyer, opens the door, gives a short scream to see Cissa bloodied up and ragged, and pulls Cissa into her arms.

"I'm fine, Mother," Cissa reassures her. "Really, I'm fine."

Ruth gives me a look worse than a curse or an epithet, a look that impales me where I stand. "I didn't know, Ruth," I say weakly. "I never guessed."

Cissa's cuts, abrasions, and bruises healed up without infection, for which even an atheist like me had to bless God. My abrasions too, though there might be a few scars. I bathed the wounds and changed Cissa's bandages daily. And when at last she did return to St. Elmo High School, Cissa was the heroine of the hour. So it might have been worth it to Miss Narcissa Douglass to see science in the flesh. It was not worth it to me.

For two days, like the rest of town, I watched as the sun

rose and set and the blanket of brimstone, phosphorous stink, and smoke hung over us.

Hank Beecham did not come down from the hills.

There wasn't any rain.

CHAPTER TEN

A man of Art Whickham's status and influence ought to have been spared the indignity of hives, but there's no justice in this world. Art's hives were made worse by the soot and dust which covered St. Elmo like the fur on a cat's back. Even the butter on his breakfast table lay under a thick grainy layer of ash, thanks to Henry C. Beecham, rainmaker. And Art's physical afflictions were nothing compared to the mental anxieties he endured. Moreover, there was no haven for him at home, no succor provided by his wife, who was a pale insubstantial creature, pretty in a way her sister, Ruth Douglass, could never have aspired to, but faded now, stiffened like white cake gone stale and crumbly.

Mrs. Whickham's nose wrinkled as she bit into a piece of toast with sooty butter, and she replaced it on the plate and wiped her fingers on a napkin. "I can't bear this any longer."

"Like hell," Art replied. "Suffering's the only thing you're any good at."

"Oh, how can you say such things to me? You know I'm fragile. I've always been fragile. I was fragile when you married me and—"

"Don't remind me." Art slathered sooty butter on his gritty bread. He wanted only to have breakfast behind him and get to the bank. "Maybe you should take lessons from your she-dragon of a sister. You think Ruth Douglass cries because she finds soot in the butter? Do you? Your sister is a harridan without equal, but you can bet she don't weep over the butter."

Art arrived early at the bank, before any of his fellow citizens could accost him with questions he couldn't answer. He informed his secretary he would speak to no one except for Otis McGahey, Sid Ferris, and Lew Cannon, all of whom joined him well before noon. Barricaded in Art's office was the only safe place for this quartet. The judge was especially vulnerable. After all, any old unemployed naysayer who wanted out of the cold could come sit in Lew Cannon's theater of criminal justice and civil dispute. Indeed, Lew had taken the extraordinary step of closing down his court calendar, pleading illness. Certainly, he looked ill, his craggy face gray, the eyes lusterless under bushy eyebrows, his patriarchal beard twisted into a knot at the end by his constant nervous stroking. The other three men were pinch-lipped and tense, but of the four, Lew alone seemed remorseful, and in low lugubrious tones, he waxed on: they ought never to have flouted God's wish that St. Elmo should have drought.

Art, though a practicing Mormon, had no use for God at the moment—and no use for Lew Cannon either. "I've heard enough, Lew! One more word about God and retribution and wickedness and righteousness and I don't care if you are a judge and bishop in my own church, I won't tolerate it! I mean it. Not. Another. Word."

"What are we going to do?" asked Otis. "Beecham is a liability. How are we going to get rid of him?"

"Find his contract and find a loophole and push him through it," Art retorted. "It's that simple. You're the lawyer."

"There is no contract," Otis reminded him. "It was all just sort of, well, we agreed on it, didn't we? But we didn't write up a contract, so we don't have anything to beat him with."

"He's a lunatic," Sid offered. "We could lock him up for that."

"Don't someone own that land out there by the reservoir? Get him for trespassing."

"The county owns the land."

"So get the sheriff and rout him out."

"I already been to the sheriff," Otis admitted, "and he says he won't go out there and risk his life and limb and that of his men. Who knows where Beecham is, or what's up there?"

"Then the sheriff is a dirty yellow coward and we ought to impeach him," Art declared.

"Would you go up there, Art?"

"Do you take me for a fool?"

"We should have waited for God," Lew moaned, wringing his patriarchal hands.

Light coming through the window lay in neat foursquare patches on the floor. Disconsolately, Art watched it illuminate the grit everywhere, while the rest of them fluttered and floundered and gibbered about ridding themselves of Hank and salvaging what was left of their political careers—to say nothing of the fledgling Doradel Fruit Company and Empire Lands. Scratching discreetly at his hives, Art twirled in his chair but did not contribute to the discussion. He wished profoundly he'd moved to San Juan County a long time ago, when he'd had the chance. True, San Juan was not the Mormon stronghold that St. Elmo was, but San Juan was a tidy town, with tourists and health seekers coming to breathe the air and spend the winters. Why was that? Why did their fruit companies prosper? Why could San Juan County grow oranges and lemons and plums and those big fat peaches and sell them to the East? All St. Elmo could grow was sugar beets and alfalfa. San Juan was as dry as

St. Elmo. San Juan didn't even have the railroad terminus. Why was it, then, that San Juan should have all that prosperity and St. Elmo should be cursed with squalor and drought? Art's hives burned when he thought of the prices he could have extracted from war-torn Europe for his forage crops. But instead of selling at a fat foreseeable profit, he— son of St. Elmo's founder—had been led astray by Hank Beecham, son of a drunk and brother to felons. The folly of it. The humiliation. Art wanted to kick himself. Make rain? Bah! Rain is no more to be made than sunshine. But water . . . water . . .

At that moment, Art leaped out of his chair as though struck by lightning, the answer coming to him in a single word, like the Word of God given Joseph Smith, or perhaps the gift of the truly Great White Father and pioneer visionary Brigham Young, as though Great Brigham stentoriously whisper-breathed: *Irrigation*. Art moved his lips over and around the word again and again. *Irrigation. Irrigation.*

"What is it, Art?" Otis asked. "You think of something?"

Art shook his head, stood, paced, his back to his friends, the better to hash this out. *Irrigation*. That's what they had in San Juan County. They had a canal, and the man who controlled the canal controlled the water, the land value, the prosperity of the whole region. That man could be prophet and see profit. Rain indeed. Art should have been thinking *Irrigation* all along, should have been hiring a bunch of boys just out of engineering school, boys eager to get started building and designing, boys who knew nothing beyond calipers and cubic feet, flumes and aqueducts, aquifers, while he, Art . . .

"What is it, Art?" Sid demanded. "Why are you scratching?"

"*Behold,*" quoth Lew, pointing to where the foursquare pattern of the window had lain across the floor and the desk. It was gone, the room suddenly dim. "*Such as sit in darkness and in the shadow of death because they rebelled against the Word of God. Psalm 107.*" Lew Cannon pulled at his beard.

"Holy blithering hell!" cried Sid.

"He's going to smoke us out again," Otis lamented, flushing, sweating, and paling.

And then, just like a musical note, a little ping, like a clock striking one, like a single word in Chinese: rain had struck the window. One drop. Two. Rain. A faltering rain, halfhearted, but rain. That first tiny gong of salvation. Art and Sid and Otis and Lew looked at one another, left the office, went out into the bank, where the typewriting machines had ceased their clatter and the rustle of paper, the clink of coin had stopped. Everyone in the bank moved slowly to windows, and with Art and the others, they gazed outside. Rain. Like a lady shaking out her umbrella. Rain. Like a dog shaking off his coat. Rain.

From the windows, they moved en masse to the door, threw it open. Along with the January cold came a breeze.

A breeze that brought moisture, a softened edge of damp-
ness. They stepped outside and looked up to where the skies
were thick with clouds like pillows stacked against a bedstead, a bolster full of wetness. From somewhere far away
came thunder. And from the mountains came a glint of distant lightning. And then the thunder moved in closer. Around
Art, people started to pray, including Lew Cannon, but Art
just grinned and slapped the backs of all his friends and
workers. Oh, it was the cavalry coming over the hill for Art,
all right, to rescue him from the Little Big Horn of his own
bad judgment, political damnation, and financial ruin.

The single pings on the tin awnings over the sidewalks
became a noisy clatter as the rain came down, drops the
size of silver dollars. Art and Sid and Otis and Lew joined
the rest of St. Elmo there on the street, whooping in front
of the bank, hands up, faces to the rain. People came out of
the shops and businesses. Men with lather all over their faces
stepped out of Bowers' Barber Shop. The Chinese ran out of
the laundries. Mexican, Methodist, Mormon, Buddhist alike,
they stood in the streets of St. Elmo and blessed the mud
growing under their feet. Shouts went up: "Hallelujah!"

"God be praised!"

"Rain, Lord! You give us rain!"

"Thank you, Jesus!"

"We are saved!"

And Art and Otis and Sid danced in the streets, shook

hands all around, rain running off their faces, shouting, "We got the rain! We got the rain! We got the rain and it still don't cost us a thing! We don't have to pay that bastard a penny!"

Rain fell intermittently for the next day and a half. Then it began in earnest. For a town that considered itself tropical if ten inches of rain fell per year, eight inches fell in two days in January 1917. And it didn't let up. Day after day, record rains battered St. Elmo. As the unrelenting rains continued, civic joy gave way slowly to consternation, consternation to dismay, dismay to unleavened fear and on to desperation, as the city found itself once again awash in destruction.

The railroad bridge over Dogsback Ditch—rebuilt after the 1911 flood—came down again. The track going out Jesuit Pass collapsed as the earth supporting it was gnawed away. The city was cut off, the great railroad that sustained it, idle. Country roads vanished and city streets dissolved into swift-moving currents. The sewer main broke, contaminating the domestic water supply. New Town withstood the rain—not without damage, but it stood. Some homes, including a few on Silk Stocking Row, sank visibly. The water got so deep that neither car nor streetcar could maneuver; mules, horses, and wagons could scarcely slog in the mud; commerce and supplies slowed, stalled, stopped. The few creeks that normally meandered around the county turned to rivers, chewing up everything before them; farmland turned to marshland; and the desert, far from blooming like a rose, sank into a bog.

Still, St. Elmo County might have withstood all this but for the Urquita Reservoir, which Lucius and Cissa had crossed on their hands and knees, New Year's Day 1917. It now filled and overfilled, and the dam at its mouth, never constructed to withstand this kind of torrential rainfall, this percussive and incessant pressure, broke. The Army Corps of Engineers would have wept to see their dam burst and the road vanish in an instant under millions of gallons of water, which roared into the valley below.

Swept before the flood was a herd of cows, the entire herd of the Sunshine Dairy. It happened midmorning. One of their drivers, Jess Sharp, was heading back up into the foothills when he saw the cows coming at him on a crest of high water. It was the last thing he saw. His body was later found twisted with barbed wire, caught in the branches of a cottonwood tree. The milk truck was swept miles farther, resting eventually upside down.

Houses collapsed, roofs ripped from walls, walls from floors, plaster dissolving like flour paste, old adobes returning to straw and dung, all this wreckage and ruination slamming, gathering force and rage, shattering other houses and barns and outbuildings, surging on a wall of water, which left in its wake, finally, a wall of mud. Livestock pens, fence posts, feed bins, carcasses of dead animals, windmills, wagon tongues whirlpooled in the fierce current. Bedsteads and buggies floated like paper boats, and whole citrus groves vanished like kindling. Tons of topsoil carrying the famous forage crops that were to feed starving Europe washed away, the resulting mud thick with straw, debris, and desolation. Trees were uprooted, crashed into one another, swirled into the valley. Water poured out of the hills and devoured everything in its path. People not content to save their lives, those who went back for their goods, paid with fractured skulls, broken bones, twisted limbs, punctured lungs, sometimes with their lives.

This watery charge, led by the Sunshine Dairy truck and a barrage of trees that had come down like matchsticks, swept into the St. Elmo Valley. In town, it washed over sidewalks and under locked doors. Children were hustled to the second stories of schools, where they watched their frantic elders pouring through the streets in the wake of the floodwaters. The Roundhouse Saloon collapsed like a deck of cards tossed down by God after a losing hand, killing three men and injuring ten others. In the basement of the county courthouse, jailed prisoners knee deep in rising water screamed and clanged their tin cups against the bars till they were rescued, chained together, marched upstairs to the courtrooms for safety; those accused of less than capital crimes were pressed into rescue service. Felons extended their hands to the righteous, white hands went out to black, black hands to brown ones, brown to yellow in the still-falling rain. People clinging to makeshift boats used makeshift implements to pull others from the wreckage of their lives, their fortunes, their sacred honor.

When it was over, Lucius Tipton found his Flyer had died a watery death, his lower bookshelves were inundated with mud, his office surgery was awash with debris, and Blanche was muddy from her femurs down. For a week, Lucius had scarcely been home; he slept when he could, ate infrequently, worked tirelessly by lamplight or candlelight and with inadequate supplies, worked not only in the hospital but went on foot or in borrowed wagons to the impromptu shelters and infirmaries: St. Elmo High School, the train station, the Methodist, Mormon, and Catholic churches. The Baptist church could not be pressed into service, as three walls and half the roof vanished, taking three people with them. The dead could not be buried, the living could not be comforted. Lucius worked without cessation amongst the dying, the broken, the ravaged, the uncomprehending. He watched them choke, shiver, weep, and bleed now in 1917, and he thought of Eden in 1911.

Ruth Douglass closed up the Pilgrim. Tom and Afton and their little children left their small uncertain home, joined Ruth, Mason, the widowed Lil, and her two little girls in the big house on Silk Stocking Row. Court was emphatically not in session, Lew Cannon waiting it out at his home, Bible in hand. Sid Ferris did not close down the New Town Hotel, stayed there, in fact, throughout the flood. Its luster was considerably diminished by the twelve inches of mud left in the lobby after the waters subsided. Art Whickham kept the bank open until the day the dam burst and all electricity died. Otis McGahey somehow slogged to his office on the second floor of a New Town brick building. He stood in his window and watched a parade of destruction, the music and wet confetti provided by the rain. The town he had lived in all his life lay below him: uprooted palms, bloated dead cats, streetcar track, a gazebo, a rocking horse, a breadbox, a bucket, a privy door, all covered with mud like fossils.

This was the town Hank Beecham found when, five days after the Urquita Dam burst—when the worst was over, the rains no longer pounding, diminished to a sprinkle—when his collected molecules staggered, slid, rolled, tumbled some-how into St. Elmo. He was soaked to the skin, his clothes torn, his hair matted to his skull, his hairless patchwork hands scratched and bleeding. He still carried his satchel. He flung himself into the crowded lobby of the New Town Hotel, where he jostled against the entire company of *La Traviata*, who were determined to leave St. Elmo, by boat if neces-sary. They had arrived in town on the last train to cross the bridge. Signor Federicci, shepherding his company of sing-ers, could be heard carrying on a simultaneous voluble quar-rel with the representatives of the Ladies' Culture League, who were not at all the cordial vanguard of refinement he'd once thought them. Nor were they susceptible as they had once been to his Continental charm. Indeed, Mrs. Otis McGahey herself referred to Signor Federicci as a weaseling nasty little spic.

"Signora!" cried the outraged impresario, shoving the sec-ond tenor from his path. "I am neezer weaseling nor leetle, nor a speek! I am responseeble"—the signor fluttered his r's—"for zee safety of my entire com-pan-y, and though, yes, we agree—last fall—to come here, to . . . to . . .," he spluttered. "But signora, we refuse to perform when zee roof of zee op-era house is leaking, and zee rain, zee rain!" The impresario threw up his hands.

Mrs. Otis McGahey planted herself before him like a tuba confronting a piccolo, like a Valkyrie facing down a gnat.

"We paid you gen-u-ine American money, and we expect gen-u-ine I-talian opera!"

"Signora McGahey," the impresario remonstrated, "I cannot reesk zee lives of my com-pan-y to perform in your opera house with zee roof she is leaking and will come down. Crash, no? Si! Crash. Astonishing, signora! Never een my life! The roof, she is *squealing*, signora, I hear this with my own eyes! Never, under zeez conditions, shall I—"

"Then, sir," said Mrs. McGahey, pulling herself to her full height, her enormous bosoms rearranging themselves with the effort, "you are a coward. The Ladies' Culture League, *we* are not afraid of a little rain. *We*, sir, are prepared to sit in that very opera house, to take the very risks you speak of, sir. *We* have every faith in the roof of the opera house. And the rain is letting up. I remind you again, sir, you have been paid!"

"Signora, all zee money in zee world . . . Please, signora, I beg of you, money alone—"

"Then give it back!" interrupted Mrs. Cannon, a sharp flinty woman worn down by years of living with the dour judge.

At this, Signor Federicci gesticulated wildly and spoke to the members of his opera company in rapid-fire Italian. They shouldered their dripping valises and pushed past the Ladies' Culture League, now reduced to calling out retributions—both human and divine—to fall upon Signor Federicci's head and offering further unpleasant observations on his family antecedents and his country of origin.

They did not even notice Hank Beecham edging his way around them toward the desk, where he informed the young mustachioed clerk that he wanted his room back.

The clerk, already undone by the operatic performance of the Ladies' Culture League, the impresario, and his babbling minions—to say nothing of the rains and the mud still clinging to the lobby floors and walls—confronted the gaunt, bleeding, ragged rainmaker. Hank's eyes were as blue as ice. The clerk cleared his throat severely, as though a whole chorus of frogs lodged there, excused himself, darted into Mr. Ferris's office. He returned with the news that Mr. Beecham was no longer welcome at the New Town Hotel.

"Is that how it is?"

"I'm afraid so, sir."

"I need some sleep. I need a hot bath. Give me a room."

"Mr. Ferris says—"

"Ferris!" Hank bellowed. "Ferris, you yella skunk! Bring your cowardly ass out here! You she-goat! Don't send this boy out here to do your dirty work! Get out here! Take your ballocks out the bank vault!"

Sid Ferris stepped through the door and up to the counter. His fleshy face was mottled with anxiety, and he avoided eye contact with the Ladies' Culture League, whose attention had been diverted to Hank. "You're not welcome here, Beecham."

Hank's thin lips twisted. He opened the satchel and took out a handful of soggy money, spread the wet bills across the counter. They lay there dripping. "How much? Goddamnit, Ferris! You know I don't dicker. Now, just you reach out and see how much it's going to cost me to be welcome here."

Ferris surveyed the money. Emotions dueled across his features, and finally he reached out and took several bills, quadruple the amount of a room at the New Town Hotel. Hank nodded knowingly and demanded the key. The clerk plucked it from a peg and handed it over. Hank swept up the rest of his money, jammed it into the satchel, and his feet squelched up the stairs.

Hank Beecham slept like the dead. He did not even stir at four in the morning when the roof of the opera house collapsed, fell into the waiting maw of the theater itself. He woke at one the following afternoon. He looked out the window, noted with some satisfaction the phlegm-colored skies and the light misting rain. He shaved and bathed, pulled clean clothes off the bedstead, where they had been drying overnight. He ate his usual steak, eggs, pie, and coffee in the empty hotel dining room. He smoked a cigarette. He took his satchel and walked to the bank.

The bank was open but unpopulated. A few despondent tellers worked behind the counters. Women with mops and buckets made feeble inroads against the mud. A male teller tried, in a lame sort of way, to bar the door to Art Whickham's office, to say the bank would not officially reopen till power was restored to the city, to reiterate that Hank simply could not burst into the office, where there was an important meeting going on.

Beecham towered over the teller and regarded him for a moment with the interest he might have paid a cockroach. Then he shouted over the man's head, "It's me, Whickham! I come for my money!"

Art Whickham himself opened the door. In the office were Otis, Sid, and Lew Cannon. A brace of candles stood on Art's desk, and though their light was feeble, it was still possible to see that Art's mouth was cinched tight as a string bag, that great wings of sweat showed beneath Sid Ferris's arms, that Otis McGahey was alternately blushing and paling furiously, that Lew exuded patriarchal wrath.

"I come for my fifty thousand dollars," said Hank, not closing the door behind him. "I filled your reservoir."

Art sat down behind his desk, which was mounded with papers. Wax from the four candles dripped forlornly on the piles of pages.

"It's God's judgment on us," said Lew Cannon to no one in particular.

"I filled your reservoir," Hank repeated. "All or nothing. That was the bet. I won. I give St. Elmo its rain."

"Did you?" said Art.

"You remember, I get credit for every drop of rain. I did my part. I won the bet."

"Did you?" said Art again.

"Give me my fifty thousand dollars, by God!"

"God, is it?" Art looked reverently skyward. "I thought God had nothing to do with this. I thought this was the work of . . . Don't interrupt, Lew," he snapped at the judge, whose lips were open. "Don't say a word." Art turned back to Beecham. "I thought this was your work altogether. You insisted you get credit."

"I filled your reservoir."

"Then you no doubt get credit for the dam breaking as well."

"I didn't say nothing about the dam. The dam is your responsibility. I didn't guarantee the dam, I guaranteed the rain. I won the bet. You owe me fifty thousand dollars."

"Very well, then," Art observed frostily, "we'll pay you."

"Oh no." Otis McGahey melted into a chair. "Oh no."

"Yes," Art continued, "we'll adhere to our part and give you credit for every drop of rain—every last damn drop, you hear me?—that's fallen on this valley. We'll give you credit and your fifty thousand dollars, and having done that, you will then be responsible for the claims, the damages charged against the city. People are suing us for bringing you here." Art shook a fistful of papers. "But we will give you all the credit you so richly deserve, Beecham, and you can work it out with all these unhappy people to the tune of . . . How much, Sid? How much so far? How high have we tallied the figure today? Tell Mr. Beecham."

Sid Ferris regarded a crumpled piece of paper in his hands. "Ah-ah-ah," he strangled out, "half a million." The last word had the effect of a chicken bone in his throat.

Hank Beecham's eyes strained in their sockets, his brow furrowed. His big hairless hands twitched, and he rubbed them together.

"That's right," Art concurred. "Half a *million* dollars! And that's just so far. That's just the bill from the telephone company and the Sunshine Dairy people, and that includes their cows and their delivery wagon, but it don't say anything about Jess Sharp who died, but I think his family's claim is in here somewhere." He shuffled through a stack of papers. "This here's claims from the Spivaks and Andersons and Myerses, the Logans and Hains and Fanns who lost their houses, and of course, there's families that lost plenty even if their houses didn't wash away." He struck the pile sharply. "That's all the white ones. Colored, Mex, and Chink, they're in a separate pile." Art stood and scooped his hands through the papers on his desk, lifted them, allowed the pages to flutter where they would, to the desk, to the floor. "Yes, here's Josh Herbert's bill for the Roundhouse Saloon. Five thousand dollars he wants for a place that dogs wouldn't piss in when it stood. Here's the bill from St. Elmo Title and Trust. They owned some of those other washed-away barns and buildings, all of it no better than kindling now. Worse than kindling. More useless than kindling. *Wet*." Art said this last word with particular relish as he plucked out another sheet. "Here's the bill from the Ladies' Culture League, who are suing the city for everything they paid to have *La Traviata* come here. And what was the rough estimate on the opera house roof?" he demanded of Sid without taking his eyes from Hank.

"Two thousand dollars," Sid snuffled.

"You'd think that roof was shingled in gold, wouldn't you? I got bills from everybody, Hank. I got niggers who want me to pay up because their barber poles and chairs are sitting at the bottom of Dogsback Ditch. I got Chinks who think I owe them new collar presses." Art swept up another armful of papers, walked around the desk, dropped it at the feet of Hank Beecham. "But all this is yours now, Hank, since you get credit for every drop of rain. We'll pay you your money and send everyone to settle up with you. Of course, if you decline to accept this"—Art paused and grinned—"then *you* owe us five hundred dollars. The advance."

The four candles on the desk sputtered. The thumping of Sid Ferris's heart could be heard over the tick of the office clock. The sweat on Otis McGahey's brow popped audibly.

"I'll see you in court," Hank snarled.

"Fine," Art replied jovially. "We'll put it on the calendar for January 1967, because it'll take that long—say, half a century—for you to get through with all these folks." He nudged the pile of papers that lay between them on the floor.

"Our agreement never said nothing about damages," said Hank through clenched teeth. "It said nothing about the dam. *Rain*. I agreed to bring the rain. All or nothing. My contract—"

"What contract?" Art's eyebrows lifted. "Otis, was there a contract drawn up and attested to?"

"No contract," Otis replied thickly.

"You can't do this to me," said Hank. "A bet's a bet. A deal's a deal."

"Of course it is." Art's lips quivered with acrimony. "We're going to live up to it. You get credit for every drop of rain. You get fifty thousand dollars and the half a million dollars in damages, the complaints and litigation lying on this desk and this floor. It's yours, your responsibility. You get all the credit. That was your caveat and we agreed to it."

"God's judgment," muttered Lew.

"Shut up, Lew! In the name of Brigham Young, *will you shut up?*" Art took a deep breath. "It has nothing to do with God. It's business. A wager, Mr. Beecham. A professional wager."

Hank Beecham took the knuckles of his left hand and wrapped his huge right paw around them; the cracks sounded like rifle reports. "You owe me fifty thousand dollars."

"And you owe everyone else. Right, gentlemen?" Art glanced at his colleagues, their faces ashen in the candlelight.

"You owe me," Hank said stubbornly. "You pay me or—I swear to you—I will take it out of this town's soul. I swear I will. I'll curse St. Elmo. I will . . ." He licked his dry lips. He began to nod his head, as though agreeing with some secret dialogue, some conversation conducted inwardly, a voice—perhaps Eulalie Beecham's—that kept its own dry counsel. He looked from face to face: Art, Otis, Sid, Lew. Keeping his eyes on the men before him, Hank Beecham reached out and brought the palm of his hand down on the four candles, snuffed each of them, acting without haste or grandeur, one at a time, till they were all out. Then he turned and left the office, leaving the four men in the smoke from the extinguished candles and the grainy gray light of a watery afternoon.

NOVEMBER

1924

CHAPTER ONE

There could be little doubt that St. Elmo had joined the twentieth century, maybe even the Jazz Age. Indeed, more than one jazz musician taking the train east to Chicago or west to Los Angeles found himself temporarily marooned here and played the St. Elmo speakeasies for money to move on. Included among these was a slender young piano man with fast hands, a slow drawl, and a diamond in his front tooth who called himself Jelly Roll Morton and who introduced St. Elmo to "The King Porter Stomp."

On his daily morning rounds, Doctor Tipton drove through downtown, once known as New Town. The old tin awnings and dry goods emporiums had given way to solid commercial establishments in stucco, buildings designed by Los Angeles architects, structures which echoed the train station's Moorish antecedents, abounding with graceful arches, cool arcades, and a few courtyards landscaped—rather than merely set about—with oleanders and crepe-myrtles, which could stand the infernal heat. Downtown, horse troughs and hitching posts were a thing of the past, as were the horse turds that used to dry in the streets, as were the horses themselves. Fords like Doctor's now snapped along at fifteen miles an hour on streets that had narrow parkways down the center and telephone poles and power poles and paved walks on either side.

On these sidewalks, Doctor noted pleasantly this November morning, there strolled women in high-heel shoes and silk stockings, light skirts brushing their knees. It was a sight Lucius relished. No one could possibly feel nostalgia for the old insular St. Elmo, except perhaps those Mormons believing in some bygone era of godliness when women were decently covered up and bonneted. Not a bonnet in sight nowadays. Now, women wore cloche hats over bobbed hair. Cissa Douglass had been entirely right about the New Woman.

Of Cissa, Lucius had always said, *Give that girl credit for audacity*, but in his opinion, for a New Woman, Cissa had certainly succumbed to the Old Story, making her way through the world by, for, and with men. In 1917, she had eloped with a boy who blew in from southern Utah with money and instructions from his family to buy farm equipment. Together, they squandered his family's entire savings on a San Francisco honeymoon memorable in every way. However, when the young couple reached Utah, the groom's family did not welcome the bride with bobbed hair. Three years later, Cissa ran off with a pan peddler, then married him eventually. By 1924, she was living in Salt Lake City, and her letters to her mother bemoaned the pan peddler's financial inadequacies and suggested that a plumbing contractor was currently soothing her marital woes.

As Lucius's Ford turned into Nauvoo Avenue, the wail of a freight train split the dry morning air. The railroad was still crucial to the valley, more so now that citrus-industry profits came from thousands of heretofore worthless acres, land rendered fertile by irrigation. The very thought of a rainmaker would have made people laugh in 1924. The flood and destruction of 1917 were a dismal memory, distant as the Battle of the Somme, dreary, antique, remote as "The Bonnie Blue Flag" in a town addicted to "The King Porter Stomp." The past had vanished. Even the erstwhile opera house now served as the Dream Theatre and showed flickering moving pictures in the dark.

Returning downtown from Afton Lance's (three of her tumultuous brood had the mumps), Doctor drove along Silk Stocking Row. Ruth continued in her big house there, living alone now. But the Row was no longer the enviable address it had once been. The pointy Victorian homes had the fatigued and moribund air of matrons in crinolines, corsets, and curly ringlets while everyone else wore short skirts and bobbed their hair. Art Whickham's family had deserted Silk Stocking Row in 1920. He had moved to a new neighborhood with ample lawns and an adjacent golf course and country club—a former alfalfa field—all of this greenery and grandeur made possible by irrigation. The streets there sported old English names like Broadmoor and Havenhurst and Crofton, but the homes recalled an almost wholly fictitious Spanish past. Art's home was of pink stucco, two stories with a red tile roof, graceful arches everywhere, inside and out. The patio in the back, complete with fish pond (complete with fish), was surrounded by large-leaved banana trees and vines of crimson bougainvillea. Outside, the Whickhams were strictly up to date. Inside, Art's wife's taste still ran to lugubrious Victorian.

Art didn't care. He spent as little time as possible at home, lavishing himself at the bank, at the offices of the flourishing Doradel Fruit Company, happiest in the company of the engineers employed by his Empire Land and Water Company. Art felt quite bracing and masculine, a regular Rough Rider in a pair of leather boots and jodhpurs, walking the various diggings, watching crews lay the flumes, secure the piping, fit the water mains that tapped the valley's artesian wells. With this broad and well-planned system of flumes and aqueducts, the Empire Land and Water Company irrigated not only the many Doradel citrus groves but also the groves of anyone else who had the money to pay for water. And pay well. Empire Land and Water controlled virtually all irrigation in the St. Elmo Valley, its monopoly accomplished completely legally in a friendly courtroom presided over by Lew Cannon. So friendly was the court that the devastation of 1917 had been legally designated an Act of God. Thus, no one was legally responsible for the damage—or for hiring the rainmaker who had provoked that damage. Before Lew's court—indeed, before the world—Otis McGahey represented the Empire Land and Water Company and the Doradel Fruit Company. McGahey's new Spanish-style house, very like Art's, boasted not only a fish pond but the first swimming pool in St. Elmo as well. Sid Ferris, despite sharing in the Empire Land and Water profits and moving to Broadmoor Street, had not fared as well as his compatriots. In 1919, Prohibition had dealt his hotel a killing blow.

Of the old quartet, only Lew Cannon's home still stood on Silk Stocking Row, and as Lucius drove past it on his way from Afton's, he noted the barbaric emblems of death festooned on the sad narrow porch. Lew Cannon was dead. They had buried him this morning. There was a black wreath on the door and black rosettes on the porch posts and the gate. The very window shades were half drawn, like the drooping gaze of some antiquated mourner.

Lucius himself was visibly more antiquated, grayer, a bit less spry, more portly, the creases at his eyes deeper—but those hazel eyes had not lost their brightness and their unceasing interest in the world. His work continued to be a source of satisfaction, inquiry, and reward; he had a fine library, the out-of-town papers, and the love of Ruth Douglass. The atheist doctor and the Mormon widow, without ever saying *I Do* before the usual witnesses, had indeed kept vows, stayed true in sickness and in health, for richer and for poorer, for better and for worse. The departure of Ruth's children, as they married and left home, had granted the widow and the doctor a pleasing frequent intimacy. Some nights after the town had turned out its lights, Doctor drove to the alley behind Ruth's house, drove his Ford into the former horse shed—now the garage—pulled the doors shut behind him. He walked through the garden and followed the back path up toward the kitchen, where he could see a light in the window and often Ruth, her long gray hair in a braid, working at the table. On these occasions, Lucius always blessed his profession; a doctor might be out and about, might be seen driving home well before dawn without raising an eyebrow or rousing an inquiry.

One would never have guessed by Ruth's demeanor when he entered the Pilgrim for lunch that afternoon that Doctor had slept by her side the night before. Ruth, as ever cool and crisp, maintained a vigilant post behind the cash drawer. A Chinese waiter—son of the original waiter—showed Lucius to a table, where he ordered immediately; he knew the menu by heart. The Pilgrim too had made the transition into the Jazz Age. Ruth Douglass made the only Green Goddess salad dressing in the whole St. Elmo Valley, and no one else could even spell *Napoleons*, much less make them. Moreover, she experimented with an odd fruit called an avocado.

Lucius leaned back and surveyed the restaurant. At a nearby table were Art Whickham, Otis McGahey, Sid Ferris, and their wives. The men wore black suits and black armbands; the women were equally somberly attired—black dresses, black hats, black gloves draped across their ample laps. They had come from Lew Cannon's funeral. Lucius was no slave to convention, but death obliges certain observances, so he pushed his chair back and ambled toward the table where they sat. "My condolences about the judge," Lucius said, addressing the group rather than a particular person.

"His like will not be seen in the valley again," replied Otis McGahey, quoting from the eulogy he had just delivered. "A man among men. We shall look in vain for another Lew Cannon."

"Amen," said the three women in unison.

"I'm sure the judge's funeral was well attended," Lucius observed.

"Everyone who is anyone was there," Mrs. McGahey retorted.

"Well, I guess death is the price we pay for life, and grief the price for loving. My respects," Lucius replied, returning to his own table, where the Chinese waiter had set his lunch.

When Lucius finished—after indulging in a Napoleon with his coffee—he paid at the front, where Ruth still sat. She inquired after Afton's sick children, but Lucius's response was cut short because Art Whickham came up right behind him. Art always bristled with efficiency, making people believe in the great things he had yet to do, while they just stood there shilly-shallying, jaws flapping, inefficiently interested in their fellow mortals.

Toothpick stuck complacently in his teeth, Lucius meandered outside and toward the Ford in the thin November sunlight, his mind on the mumps cases, when suddenly he stopped. He sniffed the air, looked skyward. Across the cloudless blue expanse drifted a long black plume of smoke, two or three of them, in fact. They seemed to unite at a central black groin and waft in a single stinking ribbon from the north. Lucius took the toothpick from his lips. Sniffed again. "Great galloping gallstones," he all but whispered.

Just then the Whickham party of six exited the Pilgrim, and as the men were escorting the ladies to the cars, Art Whickham stopped in midstride, glanced skyward. "Jesus, Joseph, and Emma!"

"Mr. Whickham!" his wife scolded.

Art (as usual) ignored her, turned to his male companions, whose noses were likewise twitching, their eyes scanning the smoke scar cutting across the sky. Indeed, much of St. Elmo was on the street at that moment, and all had their chins tilted, their noses twitching.

"Goddamnit," muttered Sid Ferris, who, as a Methodist, was less constrained than the Mormons. "Goddamnit."

Art glanced from the sky to Lucius Tipton, and wordlessly they exchanged a look. Deserting their wives, Sid and Otis followed Art as he marched up to Lucius. "Is he back? You befriended that Son of Perdition. Is he back?"

"Smells that way," snapped Lucius. "I don't imagine anyone who lived through January 1917 is likely to forget that smell. You gentlemen tell me, is Hank Beecham back? Everyone knows he vowed revenge when you cheated him out of fifty thousand dollars."

"We couldn't pay, certainly not then," Otis protested, wiping his flushing face with a handkerchief. His speech was thick and hurried. "Not with the litigation pending. I'm certain I made that clear. There was the question of fiscal responsibility resulting from the flood and the dam bursting. All that had to be resolved in the courts."

"And didn't Lew Cannon resolve it?" Lucius demanded. "Didn't he absolve you all and call it an Act of God?"

"Lew's lucky he's dead, lying in the grave, not a care in

the world," Sid moaned. "Oh, if Lew was here now, if Lew could see this, what would he say?"

Lucius tossed his toothpick in the street. "He'd say Hank Beecham has come back to St. Elmo to extract the revenge he promised. Everyone knows that's what he said before he vanished. You cheated him. Fifty thousand dollars." Doctor Tipton watched the smoke coil across the sky, "You made him a bet and you refused to pay up. Caveat emptor. Let the buyer beware. Whatever Hank does now . . ."

But Lucius did not finish his thought. He could not bear to. He had seen firsthand what Hank had planned for St. Elmo even before cursing the town, even before he vowed to take his fee from St. Elmo's soul. Appalled then, Lucius despaired now.

CHAPTER TWO

He was back, all right. No one had seen him or
heard him come into St. Elmo (which shouldn't
have surprised us, because no one saw or heard
him leave in 1917 either, heard only of the curse he'd laid
on this town when he left us knee-deep in muck and mud,
water and waste). But we didn't need to see him. We knew
by our noses Hank Beecham was back, and there was talk of
nothing else. People come up to me all that day, *Doctor, Doctor, what's that rainmaker doing? What is he going to do to this town,
Doctor?* And even when I say, *Don't ask me,* they do. Like I am
somehow implicated in what Hank Beecham does.

To give Art Whickham and his cronies credit, they drove

out that very afternoon to shut Hank Beecham down. The three of them, the sheriff, and a bevy of deputies armed with writs and orders and guns drove out in their cars, followed that plume of black smoke to its (so to speak) fountainhead, hoping like hell it was on county land and they could rout him pretty easy. But their hopes dimmed with every mile, following that smoke to its source. They all knew where it was from. Shiloh.

Though it was afternoon, the sheriff, deputies, Art, and all of them had to have their headlamps on to get through the smoke and pall as they drew closer in on Shiloh. They could see him there, an Enfield across his lap, black as an imp from hell, sitting on a wooden bench under the tin awning of the two-room shack. This house (or what was left of it) sat squarely in the center of three high towers and three cooking cauldrons, set in the same semicircle formation I'd seen in 1917. The phosphorous-and-sulphur smell was just a killer, and everywhere there were chicken carcasses. Those chickens that had dropped dead from the fumes, they all lay where they fell. The living ones were crazy and noisy with fear. It wasn't a pretty sight.

At least that's what a couple of the deputies, Floyd Sharp and Al Hinton, put round when a bunch of us gathered that evening at Bowers' Barber Shop. Grief Bowers was there, though his son and nephews do the barbering now. Grief looks after another business, one that sprung up in 1919.

Prohibition, which so crippled up Sid Ferris, made Grief Bowers a rich man. In 1922, he quietly bought out the whole building where he'd once just rented the barbershop, and he personally subscribed a thousand dollars to the building fund for the African Redeemed Church of the Lamb, which now has its own place of worship. Grief made his fortune bottling up Nana Bowers' old Majic Bitters Tonic, correctly named, if I say so myself. Nana Bowers had a healer's touch and a showman's eye, and I reckon her Tonic to be about ninety proof. And it don't taste bad either, though it isn't Burning Bush. Grief supervised the concoction of Majic Bitters Tonic at some undisclosed location and sold it out of the back room of the barbershop. Grief Bowers and Majic Bitters Tonic might be said to have ministered to this entire town (including the law).

Grief would have profited by Prohibition even without Majic Bitters Tonic, because with the bars and saloons closed down, what was left for a man? A workingman wants something at the end of the day, a place that can offer him some company and a convivial drink. You can't get that at a speakeasy, where it's all groping dark and everyone's grimly determined to have a good time and there's no solidity at all, everything to be swept away at a moment's notice if there's a raid. If you wanted more than a drink and solidity, if you wanted female comfort, that too had vanished, because the triumphant, bluenosed, sanctimonious Puritans (convinced that denying everyone liquor would keep men true to their wives and chaste before marriage) had destroyed the old Pleasure Palace. And with the loss of the Pleasure Palace went the old prospects—illegal, immoral perhaps, but essential just the same for most men—a hot bath, warm light, a soft bed, uncomplicated laughter, music, camaraderie, a girl who would sweetly sing "Kathleen Mavourneen" by the piano in her knickers. (The proprietress herself told me that. I used to do rounds out there. That was the song and the girl men most asked for.) Nowadays, the girls all work closeted singly in little cubicles, taking men back to rooming houses, to beds lit by a single electric light overhead, everyone running greater risk of disease for fewer pleasures and, no doubt, lesser profits.

So for those of us less desperate men, where could we go but Bowers' Barber Shop? Grief had expanded, and it had electric lights, a marble counter, sparkling mirrors, a tile floor, leather seats on all the chairs, a nice gingery scent in the air, glass shelves sparkling with tall bottles. And there was the back room. Majic Bitters Tonic came in bottles just the right size for the pocket of a workingman's coat. It was, all in all, a real comfortable place.

Grief and the Bowers men did a brisk business that night as, oh, maybe fifteen, twenty of us gathered there listening to Floyd Sharp and Al Hinton (both boys I brought into this world) tell their story. Floyd and Al were young and strong, veterans of the Great War, decorated for bravery at Belleau Wood, but old enough to remember the flood of 1917. In fact, Floyd's father, Jesse, was the dairy driver killed by the flood, so they had no love for Hank Beecham. But to be honest, they had no love for Art or Otis or Sid either. No, the way those boys (and most of the rest of us men gathered there) saw it, Art and Otis and Sid and the late judge were responsible for Hank Beecham's being back in St. Elmo. But you don't need the mind of Aristotle to guess that Art and Otis and Sid didn't see it that way.

Rounded out and put straight, Floyd and Al's story went like this.

Once at Shiloh, they came upon Hank Beecham. They got out of their cars in the swirling smoke and stench, the sheriff and his deputies making their way, armed through the burning pall. Floyd Sharp, decorated for bravery when he was only twenty, told those of us gathered at Bowers' that just walking toward that shack and running his tongue over his lips, the taste of grit and gunpowder, shoved him, face down, into the past, into the trenches. No Man's Land. Al Hinton said all that was missing at Shiloh was the Hun. There wasn't any Hun.

But there was an enemy.

Hank, looking old, sparse, notes pinned up and down his suspenders, sits there beneath the tin roof, Enfield rifle across his lap, not even rising when they move in on him. Sheriff calls out, "You! Henry Beecham. What are you doing out here?"

"Just taking the evening air on my own porch like any other man."

"Where's your nephew? Get out here, Earl! Earl!" Sheriff calls into the smoke.

"You want Earl?"

"I don't want Earl, damnit! I want those stinking fires put out. I want you off this property and out of this county!"

Hank looks thoughtful. He gestures with the Enfield to the men, all armed, all standing right by their headlamps. "I want you men off this property. All of you, or I'll blow you off. I want you off Shiloh. The family plantation," he adds fondly.

Sheriff declares the property belongs to Earl Beecham, who had inherited it on the death of his father, Horace.

Hank calls out for Earl, who stumbles through the door of the shack. Eyes red, jaw slack, uneasy on his feet, face all streaked with soot and smoke, like Hank's. Earl's drunk as a skunk and desperate for a cigarette, but unequal to the task of rolling one himself. Hank rolls it, neat and swift, hands it to him, lights it even. Earl lolls there, smoking, a great big grin on his face, a grin like a cougar picking his teeth with kitten bones.

"Earl," says Hank, "these men want to know who owns Shiloh."

"Why, you do, Uncle Hank. I quitclaimed it." Earl starts to laugh, so drunk he has to lean against a rickety post to hold himself up. "I give Shiloh to my uncle Hank Beecham."

"Sold," says Hank. "I been given nothing. Sold."

"That's right!" Earl crows. "Sold for cash money!" And with that, Earl starts pulling money out of his pockets, but the bills spill, start to blow away like little green tumbleweeds, and Earl falls to the ground on all fours scrambling after them, stuffing them back in his pants, all the while gibbering about one thousand dollars cash money.

One thousand dollars! Everyone in Bowers' Barber Shop, we breathe deep and whistle it back out. *One thousand dollars!*

While Earl's crawling after his money, he laughs and whoops and tells everyone he's going to Mexico with his thousand dollars, to Tijuana, where the food and the whiskey are hot, Tijuana, where a man can drink genuine whiskey and not piss brewed by slaves.

Grief, his son, his two nephews, and a cousin, they stiffen at this. You could feel it more than see it; their faces stayed still. All of the rest of us, we get prickly. Floyd, though, he meets it head on, looks right at Grief and says he's just telling what Earl Beecham said. And the Beechams, everyone agrees, are a low, vile, illiterate race of drunken dogs. Always have been. Always would be.

Except for Hank, I remind them. *Hank doesn't drink.*

Once Earl had collected up his money, he tells the

sheriff and the boys, anyone who would listen, how he's going to buy a racehorse and a race whore. "The best of both. Ride 'em till they drop," Earl cackles. "A fine racehorse and a fine-looking woman, gonna have 'em both. Gonna have it all. Turkish cigarettes too," he adds, flipping the butt into the yard. He does a little jig, dancing out toward the deputies. "So long, Hank," Earl calls out. "Shiloh's yours now, and you're welcome to it." Earl guffaws and salutes his uncle. "Yessir, General Cleburne, sir, you blow Shiloh back to the hell it come from."

Who's General Cleburne? one of the boys in the barbershop wants to know.

I look at Grief and he looks at me. We are the only ones here old enough to know, and even we can't remember Shiloh. Who can? No one in this room was even born in 1862, even me, and I am the oldest man here. Suddenly, I feel old. I tell the boys, *Patrick Cleburne was a Confederate general. He fought at Shiloh.*

Floyd tells us how Earl, without so much as a by-your-leave, saunters over to their car and asks for a lift back to town so's he can get his racehorse. The race whore he's getting somewhere else. Women in St. Elmo aren't good enough for him.

Hank, still holding the Enfield, pulls out of his pocket a deed assigning the property, for consideration of one thousand dollars, to Henry Cleburne Beecham. He ambles over to the sheriff, hands it to him, goes back to the bench, rolls himself a cigarette.

The sheriff glances at the deed, passes it over to Floyd with orders to take it to Art's automobile and let them read it. When Floyd hands this deed to Art for inspection, Art makes some remarks unworthy of a Mormon elder. Art twists and snarls, all but works himself into a pillar of salt, but after some prodding from the sheriff, he finally admits that St. Elmo National Bank and Trust had not foreclosed on Shiloh like they'd threatened to, because in 1917, the amount owing in arrears was paid off, and right after that, a month or so, maybe, Art couldn't remember exactly, but the whole of the note against Shiloh was paid and the property reconveyed to Horace Beecham. Art, jumping mad, advances toward the shack, wagging his finger at Hank, shouting, accusing, threatening.

"He was my brother," Hank says back without any inflection at all.

"You didn't give a good goddamn for your brother!" yells Sid Ferris. "You wouldn't have walked across the street for him."

The sheriff turns to Art and says, "Didn't you never think that was strange, Art? Didn't you never ask yourself who paid the mortgage on a place where no one's done a day's work in thirty years?"

To this (and to iron out the tale, lay it smooth, not like it got told that night, circular and roundabout for the benefit of those who came in on it late), Art burbled and spluttered and said something about Horace having told him of a letter he'd got from a rich investor who was willing to pay for the land but didn't want to take title to it till he was ready to start drilling.

"Drilling for what?" asks the sheriff, looking at the smoke, the towers and cauldrons and dung and chicken carcasses, the earth so dry and brown and corrugated that even the tumbleweeds are happy to blow away. "What in God's name for?"

Art looked unlike his usual self (that is, he was pale and shaken), but by and by, it comes out that Horace Beecham had finally parted with the word *oil*. Horace Beecham had thought it was the funniest damn thing he ever heard, drilling for oil on Shiloh. Horace didn't care if the investor wanted to drill for milk and honey.

And again, the sheriff inquires of Art (this time real patiently), "Didn't that never strike you as *strange?*"

Well, of course, those of us in Bowers' Barber Shop, we snicker and snort. We know that Art Whickham judged everything and everyone by his own mean mercenary standard, and amongst ourselves, we rattle back through recent memory and put some dates together, and it comes upon us like a burst appendix: to Art Whickham, the phrase *drilling for oil* would not pass unnoticed, because Art had sent his own man out and about, an Empire Lands man with a college degree. This engineer and his team, they didn't find oil but found instead artesian wells under Shiloh, under the land everywhere adjacent to Shiloh. And in a place like St. Elmo, water is as good as oil. Better. We shuffle and grunt amongst ourselves. Someone brings up how all the acreage flanking Shiloh, the original section of land Jeremiah Beecham homesteaded, everything but those few acres and the actual house (now shack), most all that ground had been bought up over time by the Empire Land and Water Company. These acres, leased to the Doradel Fruit Company, are irrigated, and now citrus groves line up out there, nice and neat, just twinkling with fruit and profit.

But the way Floyd and Al tell it, Art managed to get round the sheriff's question without quite admitting to any of this. Then the sheriff says, "Didn't you never think to look where the money came from, Art?"

"Of course I did!" Art barks back. "I never dreamed Hank Beecham would pay it! Hank Beecham hated his brother! Hank hated Shiloh!"

"Where did the money come from?" asks the sheriff, patient like he's dealing with a child.

"From someplace up north," Art whines. "Someplace up in the Sierras. I got out the map, I tell you. I held those checks in my hand and I got out the map and I found it. Someplace up in the Sierras, someplace they got snow ten months a year and a snowpack fifteen feet deep, someplace they wouldn't have any more need of a rainmaker than they would of a windmill. Someplace where there was gold! I never dreamed of Hank—"

Just a minute, I say to Floyd and Al, pushing past Ed Jessup to get closer to the chair where Floyd is having his hair cut. *Just a minute. Did Art Whickham say* where *up north? Did he give the name of the town in the Sierras?*

Did he, Floyd? Al Hinton muses.

Something with money in it, or anyway something that would make you think of money.

Paydirt. Paydirt, California.

I sink slightly, and one of the boys in the barbershop gives me his chair, and they ask if I'm all right. Grief's grandson gives me a glass of water with a nip of Majic Bitters Tonic in it. I look around me and I realize I am an old man. The boys who were throwing erasers and writing dirty words on the blackboard the day Miss Emmons vanished from the schoolroom, those boys are not just grown up but middle-aged men by now. Some of them very likely are sitting right here in Bowers' Barber Shop. But I am the only one who knows why Miss Emmons left. I am the only man in town who knows that Miss Martha Emmons, sorry spinster that she was, bolted St. Elmo and went off to marry a man fifteen years her junior (maybe more). But I keep my thoughts to myself and sip the diluted Majic Bitters Tonic, wishing it was a full-bodied swig of Burning Bush. I assure them I'm all right. *Finish up your story, boys.*

Presently, the sheriff turns to Hank and says, "Well, Beecham, this here may be your own private property, but we got laws against public nuisance, and those towers of yours, those cauldrons are a public nuisance, and I got to disarm you and ask you to shut them down. Floyd, you go get his gun."

Hank rises, slow and deliberate. He kicks open the door of the shack and points the gun, not at Floyd but inside the shed.

Floyd takes the white apron off and turns to all of us in the barbershop and near-whispers, *You wouldn't believe it, men. You wouldn't believe what he had stacked in that shed. Even from where I stood, I could see he had enough in the damned shed to destroy the Hun all over again. It looked like Belleau Wood all over again. It looked to me like he was ready to fight all of Pershing's army. And he don't ever raise his voice, just says if I take one step closer, he'll fire. He'll blow us all up. Every man jack of us. It don't matter to him. He's ready to die where he stands.*

Neither Floyd nor anyone else ventured a step toward the shack. But Floyd and Al, they hadn't been soldiers in the Great War for nothing. Floyd said he was willing to retreat, to let Beecham see them retreat. Then at night, under cover of darkness, they'd come back, flank the place all round, use the Doradel groves as cover, attack Hank from the rear. But it's like Hank had a second sense of these things. (And though I didn't say so, what did Floyd expect? Hadn't Hank been raised on tales of Patrick Cleburne and Cleburne's maneuvers, and weren't some of Cleburne's situations just as desperate as Hank's was now?)

Hank hollers out to them, "I hope you're not thinking of any flanking tactics here at Shiloh, not planning any night raids, thinking you can come in on me from the north with a surprise attack. Because if you're thinking that, well, you better bid your men goodbye, and you better tell them to say their farewells to their wives and children, because for your men, it'll be their last night on earth."

Hank says no more, and finally the sheriff just can't stand the silence and says, "Well, why?"

"I got the place mined real good. I got pickets all over the old campground, but my pickets are all underground. My sentries are all explosives, all primed, and lots of little caps and triggers you'll never see, 'cept from heaven when you get there. If you get there." His hands tightened around the Enfield. "You been forewarned. My camp is fortified, and there'll be no surprise attacks on Shiloh. One wrong step and your men die."

Well, the sheriff and Art and Sid and Otis, they threatened some more after that, blustered and blathered and rampaged on, said Floyd and Al, even tried pleading and reason, but it all came to naught. Hank wouldn't move and he couldn't be moved. He quit talking.

So it was back to town for the lot of them, retreating from Shiloh, failing for the moment, but swearing to Hank they'd stop him somehow. Floyd and Al tell us the sheriff wants to call in the military, let them go after Beecham, that it's a military situation and not the county's problem.

I left Bowers' Barber Shop after that, even though the story (especially the juicy parts about Art Whickham) was about to get retold and refashioned, probably some richness and texture added all around. But I had heard enough. I button my coat up against the November chill. I step into the street and walk to my Ford, get in, start for Ruth's. I wonder if Art Whickham remembers Miss Emmons.

Miss Emmons . . . Miss Emmons . . . All I can muster of Miss Emmons is a tiny woman (no ankles showing, no sir, and no bobbed hair), a high-collar-clad woman dressed in brown, brown hair, brown eyes, brown as a mouse or cockroach or some other such insignificant creature. Brown with flecks of gray in her hair and a mouth cinching tighter with every passing year. How old was she when she ran off to marry Hank Beecham? If not forty, at least so close she could have smelled forty. I could not remember what she looked like, but I could imagine the wedding, if not the marriage. Miss Emmons probably stood with her former student in front of some justice of the peace, a man with gravy stains on his vest, his dried-up wife for a witness, his supper getting cold in the next room. And I could picture the divorce. Hadn't Hank himself told me the story? How Miss Emmons told him he had broken her heart, and wished he'd had one to break. How Miss Emmons went back to teaching for the rest of her life. How she preferred earning her bread before snotty boys and pouting girls in Paydirt, California, to taking money she might lawfully have had from Hank.

I could not altogether picture Martha Emmons, but Eulalie Beecham, she came back to me. Clearly. Her taut face, cold blue eyes, her tough hand shaking mine thirty years ago. More than thirty years. Eulalie came back to me: *I'll never forget this, Doctor.* And for a moment, her voice melds into Hank's: *You'll never forget this, Doctor.* And I understood his return, and it was certainly not the money. Maybe St. Elmo had forgot the flood of 1917, forgot 1917 altogether, forgot the Somme, forgot Verdun, forgot Shiloh and Chickamauga and Missionary Ridge and all the rest of those places where men suffered and bled and died for Lost Causes. Lost or gained, what did causes matter to the dead? And the living? They forgot and moved on, like St. Elmo had rebuilt after 1917, busied themselves with Life, Liberty, the Pursuit of Progress, the making of money, and nary a thought to the past. Hank had not forgot. He was Eulalie's son, and in 1916, he had returned to St. Elmo to redeem Eulalie's lost causes, the things she had lost or never had, to restore the honor that Jeremiah had beat out of her, to reverse the contempt she'd endured as a Beecham. And Hank would do all this with a glorious achievement: his skills against nature. And for this glorious achievement, St. Elmo would dignify—with cash—the suffering Eulalie had endured and grant his mother a measure of respect she had never known in life. In this undertaking, he had been thwarted, defeated, outsmarted by the very men who had despised her all along. We should have expected him back again. I should have, anyway. Maybe I did. But I would not have expected him to pay on Shiloh. To pay it off, in fact. And somehow (blast me if I could figure it, I couldn't), he'd got Miss Emmons to conspire in this. Now, it only remained to be seen to what purposes Hank would put this land. Would it be enough for him to scare us into submission, to have St. Elmo come crawling out to Shiloh, fifty thousand dollars in hand? It was never the money to Hank. No one knows that better than I. After all, I was out there in 1917. I saw him. One man of science to another. Maybe I am implicated in this. Maybe I understand what the rest don't. Can't say I admire or condone it, but . . .

I stopped the Ford right there in the middle of the street, let it chug and idle while I debated, and then, even given the lateness of the hour, I turned the car around and headed north toward Shiloh.

I got lost a couple of times going out there, but I found it finally. I had not been there since the night Virginia Beecham needed me. From the moment the sound of my Ford might have been detected, I saw a window light up in the shack at the end of the road, and the door was flung open, and through the smoke and pall, I could see, framed there, Hank Beecham, Enfield in his arms and the sights leveled on me.

Waving my white handkerchief out the window, I hollered over and over, "It's me, Hank! Lucius Tipton!"

Pulling in closer, I could see he'd set the three towers in a semicircle not too far distant from the shack, and fires still burned under the cauldrons. I scrutinized the place as best I could by the Ford's headlamps, but it didn't look to me that there was any sundial of dynamite as yet, no giant fan with incendiary ribs like I'd seen in 1917. So it seemed there might still be time, and I took hope and heart.

"Don't waste your breath!" Hank called out, but he lowered the Enfield.

My lungs hurt and my eyes and nose stung, so thick and smoky was the air, but I killed the motor and stepped out. I could hear the wind whistling around the lapsed corners at the back of the shack, the part that had fallen down. I called out that I had come by myself, but he did not reply, remained motionless, filling up the doorway. "It's not the money, is it, Hank?"

"Not anymore." He turned and walked into the shack.

I followed him, walking through the ashen expanse of the yard, where the bodies of dead chickens lay, the wind disrespectfully ruffling their feathers, altogether in keeping, I thought, with a place where every hope and any endeavor had long since languished and died. Inside, Hank wiped clean a smoky glass and lit another lamp. A tiny fire flickered through the grate of a small cookstove. He nodded to me to take the single splintered chair, and he sat down on what had been Earl Beecham's narrow bed and rolled himself a cigarette.

In the frail light, I could see that Floyd and Al were right:

there was enough here to fight the Hun. Boxes of dynamite were stacked along the wall, and kegs of gunpowder lined up smartly. In parade formation across the small table and beneath it stood the same implements I'd seen in 1917: regiments of jars and vials, brigades of measuring spoons, ladles of every variety, paper and sticks for rockets, a scale with its weights. The same smells (linseed oil, pitch, camphor gum, resin) haunted the place. And of course, there was the heavy granular presence of gunpowder. There were no rubber boots in evidence. No goggles. Otherwise, it was all as I remembered, the scale of the assault diminished but the same intent intact.

And Hank, was he the same man he'd been eight years ago? For a man who stuck to the essentials, Hank Beecham had been purged of everything that was not, as though he'd been through the refiner's fire, like metal from which every alloy has been burnt off, leaving only what is hard and pure. Like his eyes. His eyes were still hard and pure, but his eyebrows and mustache, those were gone, and his hair had retreated across the open plain of his skull. Such hair as remained was ash colored, long, unkempt. His unshaven cheeks were gray. The very flesh had deserted his bones. The skin on his harlequin hands pulled, stretched like fleshy rags unequal to the task of covering his enormous knuckles. His jawbone seemed whitened, pronounced as Blanche's mandible, but even at that, I could tell the jaw itself had deteriorated, giving his features an irregular, off-center look. It was an affliction I had never seen personally, but I'd read of it, a condition suffered by workers in match factories. Phossie jaw, they call it. Phosphorous necrosis. There is no cure.

"Say what you have to say and leave."

"I'm here one man of science to another."

"I'm not a man of science anymore."

"Then what are you?"

"General Cleburne, maybe," he replied absently, moving his feet back until they hit a couple of bottles. Earl Beecham's legacy, I reckoned. Distastefully, Hank pulled them from under the narrow bed, leaned over, opened the door, flung them into the night. They hit the dirt with an audible thud.

I winced at the sound. "Pretty careless, aren't you? Pretty careless for a man who's got his ground all mined."

For a moment, he pondered, crinkling the cigarette between his bony fingers. "What did you 'spect me to tell 'em, Doctor? Oh, gentlemen, by all means, attack my undefended flank and rear? They'll find out the truth soon enough." Hank shrugged. " 'Sides, if I'd really had the place mined, that Earl would be a thousand pieces. He's a fool, all right. No, I'm the only sentry on duty at Shiloh. But I'm still ready for 'em. Don't think I'm not. And I'll fight when I'm attacked."

"How long you been out here?"

"Two, three weeks."

"How'd you keep Earl from blathering it all over town?"

"Earl was easy," Hank sneered. "For a thousand dollars,

Earl would of bedded down with Ulysses S. Grant hisself. I
needed his help anyway, to get set up."

"Pretty hard to sneak three steel towers and three huge
cook pots past a whole town. How'd you do that?"

"Mail order," he replied laconically. "Nowadays, get anything you need short of a rat-catching cat out of the mail-
order catalogs. Freight prepaid." From the corner of his eye,
Hank spied the body of a dead mouse, and he used the bar-
rel of the Enfield to nudge it out of sight. "I brung the rest
of it with me. Got a Dodge truck out back of this shack. Just
like Pershing used against Villa."

"Pershing never caught Villa."

"Wasn't the truck's fault." Hank cracked his knuckles so
loud I winced on behalf of his bones.

"So you ended up owning something after all."

"I guess I did at that. Probably should have bought one a
long time ago. That truck take you anywhere. You can just
about defy nature in one of them Dodges. Defying nature's
my business."

I was tempted to contradict, to say that from what I'd
seen, Hank undertook to defy God. But instead, I asked if
he had any coffee.

"This ain't the Pilgrim, Doctor." But he hove to his feet
and went to the round-bellied cookstove, flung in a few sticks
of wood, set the tin pot atop it. "I been 'specting you. I knew
you'd come. I respect you for it. But it's a fool's errand. There's

nothing you can say to make me alter my course here, Doctor. I will not retreat and I will not surrender."

I paused and pondered where to begin, and it came to me that except for what had collapsed, Shiloh hadn't changed since I'd tended Virginia and made my pact with Eulalie. However much the rest of the world had altered, here time had stilled unto stopped. Perhaps if Hank could be pulled from this place, he could be pulled from the past. "St. Elmo is a new place, Hank," I began. "You should come with me, walk the streets. What you remember, that's all gone. The town's changed. The world's changed, Hank. It's 1924. Women can vote now. Some people got radios. You ever seen one of those, Hank? Heard one? You can go to the pictures now, Hank, pictures that move. You can sit right there in the Dream Theatre and watch moving pictures." Hank remained unimpressed, expressionless, so I came in closer to home. "People got irrigation now. They don't need rain or rainmakers. They pump the water out of artesian wells. Even here at Shiloh, you got water deep under the ground. Look all around, the acreage surrounding your land, haven't you seen it? Orange groves where once there was sagebrush and tumbleweed. Irrigation did it. This place, Shiloh, it could have prospered. It could yet."

"I know all about irrigation," he replied sourly. "Nothing glorious in irrigation. No wrath. No wonder."

He moved back to the bed and took the Enfield up

gently, like you'd touch a companion. And maybe it was his companion. I had never pitied Hank Beecham and I did not do so now, but I could see that purged from him too had been any warming contact of a human hand, a human voice. All right, I thought, I'll wade right in. Frontal assault.

"Don't do this, Hank," I began gravely. "Don't. Give this town the chance to right what Art and Sid and Otis and Lew Cannon did wrong. Lew's dead," I threw in, "gone to hell or Mormon heaven. Same thing, by my reckoning. Don't judge the people of St. Elmo by Art Whickham's low standard. I'm not talking a lot of hogwash about Christian forbearance or turning the other cheek. None of that. Those people in St. Elmo, they're no different from you. You think for one minute there's a man in that town who sleeps without some old grudge or hurt gnawing at his dreams? You think there's a woman alive without some old wrong, some injury from the past that's never going to heal? You think there's anyone who hasn't got something they'll regret till the day they die? Some loss or wrong they feel so intensely they're sure it will go on living even after they die? Everyone's got something like that, Hank. You're not alone. Everyone who ever wanted something they didn't get, or loved someone they lost, or had a dream they held dear denied them, or snatched away forever." I mop the sweat from my brow; the stink and fumes in here were every bit as bad as 1917. How did he stand it? "Gallstones, man! The task of the living is not the eating and sleeping and doing your duty. The great task is that you take these dead dreams, these wrongs, these desertions, and you find some corner in your heart, some hallowed ground, and you bury them. And you get on with the living. Let the dead lie in peace."

He rested his blue eyes on me. "You really think there's peace for the dead?"

"I'm a doctor. I know that in death the body is at peace, Hank. Peace beyond all pain, beyond suffering and sensation and thought. That's a kind of peace. Beyond that, beyond the material body, I'm ignorant as the next man."

Hank rose and poured us each a tin cup of coffee. Passed me mine. The cup itself was hot, and the coffee must have been brewing for days, because it was bitter and had the grit of gunpowder in it.

"I gave this town their chance," he said stubbornly. "I filled the reservoir. I won the bet. I vowed I'd take my fifty thousand dollars out of their humpbacked souls."

I tried to counsel against it. "I'm not a vengeful person myself, Hank. I understand it, though. I don't say I condone or admire, but I understand what it does to people. I've sewed up too many vengeful men, their intestines hanging out, their arms and legs broken, faces shattered, heads split open in brawls that started over women, or slights to pride bloated with liquor. I've seen too much of it not to understand revenge, Hank. I've seen it hot and I've seen it cold, but I swear

I've never seen anything like what you're doing out here."

"This ain't revenge," he corrected me. "This is war, Doctor. No retreat. No surrender. Victory or death."

"Wars aren't that clean or clear anymore. Look at the Western Front. Look what they called war in France, and at Gallipoli. They called it the Great War, but what was great? What was won? Where's the victory? It was death. That's not victory. It was a whole generation of men just crawling through death and coming out dead. Even the living. I've seen that too," I said sadly, taking a sip of brimstone brew. "I've seen that too."

"Trenches, barbed wire, gas, make war how they will, Doctor, firepower still brings rain. In war, you can count on fire and rain." And then, as though the mention of fire cheered him, he lit the cigarette he had rolled and put the match out between his thumb and forefinger.

"Do you think Patrick Cleburne would make war on an innocent civilian population?"

Hank snorted. "You do put together a tidy argument, Doctor. But I come to collect on my bet."

"Well, Hank, for a man who sticks to essentials, that bet made no sense. Not then. Not now. It was preposterous. Fifty thousand dollars! It's enough to start your own damn country!"

Hank laid the Enfield on the floor, stepped over it to the cookstove, and warmed his massive hands. "I thought the money would of pleased Martha," he said at last. "Pleased Ma. I thought, for Ma anyway, it might of been good as curtains at the window. Flowers by the door. A stone of rosy marble. An angel at her grave. I would of done that for Ma."

"Then let us, let St. Elmo get a stone of rosy marble, an angel for your mother's grave. We can do that! We will do it! We'll do it right. We'll give your mother a marble angel. No one will ever forget Eulalie Beecham."

Hank turned back around, and something in his expression had warmed itself there at the stove, softened perhaps.

"Call it off, Hank. Put out those fires. Unload all this goddamn gunpowder."

Hank moved back to the bed and picked up the Enfield. "Genuine Union general," he said with something like levity. "No one but a fool would go into battle, buttons in one hand, epaulettes in the other, would they? Your very words, Doctor. But a fine Enfield, that's something else. I got shotguns too. Dynamite in the privy. Got my own army out there." He nodded toward the cauldrons. "Can't you see their watch fires on the old campground tonight?"

"You got a sword?" I scoffed.

"Sword's useless. I wouldn't have a sword. You could slay a whole regiment with a sword and never have rain. Gunpowder. Sulphur. Phosphorous. Dynamite. You need firepower to make rain."

"You need firepower to make war too. When I saw you

up at the reservoir in 1917, I knew you were making war on heaven, on God Himself."

"God has nothing to do with it."

"Admit it! You don't give a good goddamn about rain. If rain comes, it's the same unconscious rain that fell after Shiloh, after Waterloo, after the Somme. Just a by-product of war." I bolted the coffee and put the cup down. "You're going to die out here, Hank. Why refight Shiloh? Shiloh was sixty years ago. More than sixty years. Why die for it now?"

"Time means nothing to me."

I stood up slowly, feeling old and defeated. "Well, I guess I've wasted my breath."

"I knew you'd come, though. And like I said, Doctor, I respect your coming. But you take a message back to the enemy for me. You tell 'em, next man out here, next face I see—even you, Doctor, I mean it—I'll aim the Enfield"—he pointed it now at the dynamite neatly stacked—"and I'll pull the trigger. We'll die where we stand."

"And what if no one comes? What if they let you just starve out here in your one-man arsenal, your one-man war?"

"They'll aggress me. You know they will. They'll aggress me and I'll have to fight."

I put my hat on my head. "Why should people go on dying at Shiloh?" I implored him. "Why should you be like all the rest of the Beechams, dying at Shiloh or because of it? Let St. Elmo make it up to you. Go on living, Hank."

"You can't buy off a man who only wants one thing." Hank stood and opened the door of the shack.

"What is that one thing? Tell me."

"Victory. It's what they all wanted."

"Who? Who?"

But he motioned me out the door with the rifle, and I took my leave, walked away. But then I stopped and turned back, called to the shack. "Answer me this. How did you get Miss Emmons to make those two payments for you? Why did she pay off Shiloh?"

"Martha paid off nothing. I paid. She let me use her bank. That was all."

"That's enough, isn't it? I thought she hated you, that you'd broken her heart and she wanted the divorce forever final. Weren't those her words?"

"Her words, Doctor. Martha's very words."

"Why did she do it?"

"Time means nothing to her either."

Well, I thought, time means something to me. It might mean a lot. "Is she still up in Paydirt?"

"Probably. I don't know. Maybe. She's alive, though. I know that. If Martha'd died, I'd know it."

"I could treat that jaw problem you have," I lied.

"You better leave now, Doctor."

"You don't have to die out here, Hank. You don't have to die at Shiloh."

He leaned into the frame of the door, as though weary. "Pa used to say, that first night, after the battle, never minding the dead all around 'em, the living just feasted and roared round the Union camps they'd took. Pa said they'd sent word to Jeff Davis in Richmond of a great victory in Tennessee. They were certain the enemy was crossing the Tennessee River that very night, even though Union gunboats on the river fired shells every fifteen minutes, all night long in the rain. Shells to shriek and pound all night, so there'd be no sleep for the weary. Pa said, Hell, what did we care? They was whupped, Grant and Sherman was whupped. Pa said they could hear the Union drums and trumpets, and believed Grant and his rascals was gone, pulled out of Shiloh altogether and crossed the river. But the next day . . ." He drew his lips in a taut seam and shrugged. "Well, I guess Pa and them wished they'd got some sleep."

"It wasn't a test of valor that second day," I tried to explain. "The Confederates, Cleburne, Jeremiah Beecham, they had valor, but Grant had reinforcements, fresh troops for the second day, new men for the fight."

"Good night, Doctor. Goodbye."

I said goodbye. What else was there to say? I walked out into the night, the sky theatrically curtained with smoke, the moon and stars shut out. But there by the Ford, before I got in, I remembered something. "I forgot to tell you, Hank," I called back to the spare figure. "The court officially ruled that the 1917 flood and everything that happened in its wake, all of it was declared an Act of God. That ought to please you, Hank." I hoped for a whoop of vindication, at least a low chortle of delight, but nothing followed me as I drove away, just the sound of the wind whistling round the shack, through the three towers, breathing on the flames, the embers twinkling beneath the still-burning cauldrons.

CHAPTER FOUR

For forty years, nothing had kept Art Whickham from the bank, saving for the Spanish influenza in 1919, and that time in 1906 when a horse had stepped on his foot. Oh, and his honeymoon, which he remembered less than the horse stepping on his foot. But the day following their retreat from Shiloh, Art Whickham could not get out of bed. He was sick. He lay in the high connubial fourposter in a darkened room, drapes drawn, blankets up to his chin. He had the chills and a jumpy stomach. Wretchedness aboundeth. Yesterday morning, he'd gone respectfully to the funeral for an old and trusted friend, Lew Cannon, and by afternoon, he was at Shiloh, ankle-deep in chicken dung and ash, trying to explain to the sheriff and every peach-fuzzed deputy how he, Art Whickham—president of St. Elmo National Bank and Trust, stockholder and chairman of the Board of Directors of Empire Land and Water, partner in the Doradel Fruit Company, former mayor, elder of the Church of Jesus Christ of Latter-day Saints—how it was that he had been duped by a Beecham.

Art should have known better. And yet—he pleaded inwardly with some unseen shame—hadn't he, hadn't everyone in the bank that day in 1916, hadn't they all heard Hank Beecham say to his own brother, *I ain't paying a cent on that land?* Everyone heard him. Hank hated Shiloh. Loathed the place. Everyone knew that. Who would have ever dreamed he would pay it off? Get it reconveyed to the brother he despised? Nobody. Just the same, Art knew that to one and all, he looked a great fool. He had been duped by that Son of Perdition. And now he would be blamed for whatever calamity that Son of Perdition unleashed next.

Early that morning, Art had informed his wife in no uncertain terms that he would speak with no one, that she should not answer the door, nor should any of the servants; they were not to admit a single person to the Whickham home. She had demurred, saying that the ladies of the Relief Society had planned . . . But Art growled so convincingly that she had backed out of the room, murmuring assurances, promising she would not even answer the telephone. She had, of course. He had lain in bed and listened to her speaking into the telephone on the landing. He knew that the St. Elmo operator was hanging on her every word, that everyone in town was getting ready to pounce on Art and Sid and Otis, to blame them for the rainmaker's reappearance and his next disaster. Art twisted himself in the bedclothes, thrashing mentally and physically. Blame and rain, Art vowed inwardly, they have to fall on any head but mine.

He heard his wife enter the bedroom now, bearing a tray with a glass of milk and a bowl of egg gruel with chunks of white bread floating in it. She set the tray down in front of the vanity and was about to open the drapes when he barked at her.

Mrs. Whickham's lower lip trembled, and her spongy face seemed to reverberate with suppressed tears. "I'm doing the best I can, Art. The Relief Society ladies couldn't come anyway. They're too afraid. Everyone's afraid. What's Hank Beecham going to do, Art? What if he can't be stopped? What's going to happen?"

"Oh, shut up! I wish to Brigham I was married to your sister. You think she's wallowing in a great puddle of fear? Ruth Douglass could face down the devil. You couldn't face down a coolie. Now get out! Leave me be. I have to think."

Fist pressed to her lips, Mrs. Whickham ran from the room weeping. Art knew he'd have to make it up to her later. They had that sort of marriage. She kept him in check with her weaknesses. He kept her in check with his bullying.

Art's stomach was jumpy, but he had to eat. Getting out of bed, he went over to the tray on the vanity. Picking up the silver spoon, he brought a morsel of egg gruel and soggy white bread dripping to his lips, and just then, he happened to glance at his reflection in the mirror. There he was, Arthur Madison Whickham, youngest son of the tenth wife of the famous Mormon scout, the founder of St. Elmo, still in night-clothes at noon, slurping milksop and being looked after like a toothless, hairless, thin-shanked he-goat. "By Brigham!" Art flung the spoon across the room. "I won't have it! No! By the bowels of Brigham, I won't! Shall I be bested by Gen-tiles? No! The thought makes reason stare!" he added, quot-ing from an old Mormon hymn, his favorite.

Art flung off his nightshirt, shaved, dressed for work. But he did not go to work. He wasn't quite ready for that. He went downstairs, snarling at everyone he passed, and out back to the flagstone patio of his new home, surrounded by a lawn made green by irrigation.

He sat on a bench by the fish pond, throwing stones into it. He scratched at his hives and aimed at the defenseless fish. He hit one, stunned it, and was presently rewarded with the sight of the fish's golden body floating, belly up, in the green water. He kept trying to hit another. For hours, he thought and cast stones, and perhaps the pond held only goldfish, but as the afternoon passed, they came to be Golden

Tablet Fish. Verily. Like unto the Golden Tablets given Joseph Smith by the Almighty Himself. Sitting by the goldfish pond was not exactly forty days in the wilderness, but for Art Whickham, the result was the same, for there came unto him Revelation. In the very words of the Bible itself: *Let the dead bury the dead.* Matthew, chapter eight.

The next day's *Herald-Gazette* carried the following item.

Dear Friends and Fellow Citizens:

The stinking smoke which o'er hangs our fair Valley, and the remorseless revenge of the man responsible for that stench, result from unfortunate insistence, some years ago now, of Judge Lew Cannon. It was Judge Cannon's firm belief that a rainmaker was the answer to the Valley's problems. We, the undersigned, argued relentlessly with Judge Cannon in 1916. We fought him on this issue, our objections numerous as autumn leaves. To wit: If God wanted St. Elmo Valley to have rain, God would send it. Mortals ought not to intervene in God's will, and a rainmaker, by his very profession, interferes with God's will. We reasoned and argued with the late Judge, but to no avail. He insisted on Beecham. Nothing could quell his enthusiasm for inviting the rainmaker to St. Elmo, and reluctantly we relented.

Now, though the Judge himself is beyond Beecham's

retribution, we, the people of St. Elmo, must bear the brunt of Lew Cannon's bad judgment. Candor further compels us to admit, though we have no wish to speak ill of the dead, the bet for $50,000 was Lew Cannon's idea. All or nothing, Lew Cannon insisted. And though the rest of us believed that in fairness we ought to pay Beecham (though he had wrought destruction upon us), Lew Cannon refused. Lew Cannon would not allow us to make good the bet with Henry Beecham. In this thinking, the Judge, a well-meaning man, was guided by his concern for the sufferings of the people of St. Elmo Valley. Also, as he later ruled, the flood of 1917 was an Act of God for which no mortal should accept money.

Only the current and immediate emergency under which we all labor could wring from us the admission of the Judge's complete responsibility for this tragedy. To his widow and family, we extend our sympathies and our sorrow, the hand of fellowship and forgiveness. Lew Cannon was a Bishop of his Church, a pillar of the community, a man we all admired, however ill-informed was his decision. He was an able Solon and a convincing man, and over our objections, he invited Beecham, he made the bet, he refused to pay.

The broken dam, the roads washed away, the homes destroyed and property lost, much of that is restored now, thanks to St. Elmo's solid Republican leadership, the work of men who can count on an attentive Federal ear. Otherwise we might yet be living with destruction wrought in 1917 by that madman, Henry Beecham. If only he could have been stopped! And one man might have stopped him. Dr. Lucius Tipton was a witness that fateful day in 1917. Dr. Tipton is a well-known atheist who watched Henry Beecham fire up his devil's brew without uttering a word of protest. He allowed Beecham to wreak vile destruction upon an innocent people.

From the loins of drunkards spring madmen. Now Henry Beecham thirsts for revenge as his father thirsted for drink. There are those good citizens who can yet remember the rest of the Beechams. His sister was a horse thief. His two brothers died violently, one in prison. His father could often be found crawling on all fours or lying dead drunk in vile holes of sin and iniquity, all of which have been closed now by virtue of the Volstead Act, the Eighteenth Amendment to the Constitution, and the Noble Experiment. Prohibition will spare us watching any more lives end as Jeremiah Beecham's ended. Prohibition will protect our women, who can now walk in the streets of St. Elmo unmolested by drunks. Prohibition protects the purity of our homes, because there is no house of prostitution that can survive without the twin demons of alcohol and opium. Dr. Tipton, an atheist, has ever been known to have disapproved of Prohibition.

Our fellow citizens, though this disaster (neither this one nor the one in 1917) was not our wish, nor any of our doing, still we stand ready to help St. Elmo in its hour of need. We will do all in our power to rid the Valley of the Beechams once and for all. We will do our best to right Lew Cannon's grievous wrong.

Your obedient and humble servants,

Arthur Madison Whickham
Otis Stebbs McGahey
Sidney Franklin Ferris

CHAPTER FIVE

"If that don't beat all," I said to Blanche, *Herald-Gazette* in hand that night. "You got to hand it to them. For a bunch of desperate men, they're doing a fine job of looking like archangels, aren't they?" Blanche agreed with me. She was always real accommodating like that.

When I heard a knock at the door, I figured it would be Ruth. Ruth would be fired up and angry to see me publicly accused of conspiring with Hank Beecham to flood St. Elmo in 1917. Ruth would tell me to sue those sonsofbitches for slander, though she wouldn't say it just like that, of course. But I open the door and it's not Ruth. I could not have been more surprised if before my eyes had stood a delegation from

China, mandarin robes and all, bearing a portion of the Great Wall. It was Art Whickham and Otis McGahey. "Gentlemen," I told them, "I've no cure for what ails you."

"Doctor Tipton," commenced Otis, "on behalf of the concerned citizens of the St. Elmo Valley, we have come to you to ask your help."

Otis McGahey could have sung "Hello! My Baby" so it sounded pompous. As I'm listening to him, I peer round the door and into the dusty yard. There were just the two of them. "Where's Sid Ferris?" I ask. "Rascals always come in packs of three, don't they? I mean, after the fourth has died."

Otis, shame and dismay making him flush and stammer, looks for some oratorical way of addressing my question, but Art just spits it out. "Sid's gone. What profiteth it to lie? Sid's left town, and even his wife don't know where he's gone or when he'll be back. He's deserted and left us to face this alone. The yellow-bellied Methodist."

I scoffed at this and padded back to the study, and they followed me in. Old Blanche, protectively behind me, clattered in protest as I sat at my desk. I let the two of them rustle about as best they could amidst the books and papers cluttering the two chairs across from me. They sit down gingerly, and I get out a cigar. "I see you men are making full fine use of the freedom of the press." I point to the *Herald-Gazette*. "I ought to sue you for slander, coupling my name in print with that pious old humbug Lew Cannon."

"It's like this, Doctor," Otis began. "We are not prepared to let Hank Beecham destroy this valley again."

"You were prepared in 1917. You just weren't prepared to pay him."

"He is motivated by that most base of human impulses," said Otis.

"Which is?" I lit the cigar.

"Revenge."

"Really? You think revenge is baser than greed?"

"We didn't come here for a theoretical discussion," Art snapped.

"Then get to it, and spare me all this chloride of lime."

"We believe," said Otis with a quick glance to Art, "that you might possibly hold some sway with Hank Beecham. We believe that, given the esteem in which he holds you, you might be able to save this town."

"To save your worthless hides, you mean."

"Reputation is small consideration at this point. The 1917 flood was deemed an Act of God, but we could not have assessed that right then. Why should he revenge himself on us now?"

"For fifty thousand dollars, maybe?" I asked.

"We offered to pay it," Art replied drily. "We sent a messenger out to Shiloh with a flag of truce yesterday, and we offered to and he refused."

"Did you send cash?"

"Only a fool would send cash to a madman."

I puffed on my cigar. "You got any idea who paid Shiloh off?"

"That devil Beecham. That Son of Perdition." Art started scratching both arms.

"But," I reminded him, "you cashed those drafts on a bank in Paydirt, California, and never thought they came from Hank Beecham. You said you knew they couldn't be from Beecham. So who was it?"

"Get to the point." Art scratched furiously. (Hives, my professional guess, eczema maybe.)

"Does the name Martha Emmons mean anything?" I could tell it didn't. "You remember a day, oh, thirty years ago, more maybe, when a schoolteacher didn't show up at her classroom, left a week's rent on the boardinghouse bureau, and bolted this town?" I smoked my cigar and let Blanche glare at them. "This schoolteacher left to join Hank Beecham. Married him, in fact," I added casually, while they sputtered and coughed and looked bewildered, as they tried to resurrect the insignificant disappearance of an insignificant schoolteacher. They were still trying when I told them Miss Emmons had divorced Hank as well. And before they could collect their sorry selves, I said, "After that, she moved to Paydirt, California." I watched while they wheezed and puffed and frowned and flustered. *Martha Emmons? Martha who? Marriage? Divorce? Paydirt, California?* You could see them gasp and rattle and try, without success, to conjure up even the notion of Miss Emmons, much less the memory.

"She's your only hope," I said. "She divorced him, but she let him use her bank, to make those drafts from Paydirt, so far north you'd never guess, so Hank could hold onto Shiloh. That makes me think she still loves him. I believe he still loves her. I believe she might be able to make him change his mind."

"Are we to go to Paydirt, Doctor, and fetch her all the way down here? We could be underwater before that!"

From the rubble on my desk, I plucked out two telegrams. "I sent a wire to the school superintendent in Paydirt yesterday, and this is what I got back." I showed them. *Miss Emmons. Left district 1921. Ill health.* "So I wired again. It just might be that we have a chance to stop Hank Beecham. Read it." *Lives with sister. Agnes Kreuger. Chagrin, California."*

"Chagrin!" cried Otis. "Why, that's in this county! In the desert, the blistering middle of nowhere."

"Chagrin's closer to hell than St. Elmo, but Miss Emmons is our only hope," I maintained. "If we got a chance at all."

"Very well," said Art. "We can wire Chagrin and set up an appointment with Martha Emmons. But Shiloh is closer than Chagrin, and Shiloh's where that lunatic's set up. You go to Shiloh, Doctor. Tonight. You talk with Beecham. He respected you. Admired you. You go talk to him. You go tell him—"

"I don't need you to put words in my mouth, Art. I don't need you for anything. Besides"—I got a little prickly and flicked the ashes from my cigar into a tin cup on the desk— "I've already been to Shiloh."

They implored me over and over, each in his own way (Art all indignant, like I stood between him and some toll he was collecting, Otis like some jury hovered unseen behind Blanche), to tell them what I'd seen, what Hank had said. But I would not be pushed or bullied. I said again Miss Emmons was our only hope. But as for Hank Beecham, I gave Art and Otis the telegram version of what he'd said: *Step foot on my land, I'll aim the Enfield into the dynamite. I'll pull the trigger. We'll die where we stand.* That was all I said, because I knew that even though I must and would ally myself with these two scoundrels on behalf of St. Elmo, I would never betray Hank Beecham to them. I had formally accepted with and from and of Hank Beecham a trust I did not want, a trust, moreover, that had not even been asked of me.

The St. Elmo Valley sprawls at the mouth of a natural navigable corridor through the mountains—Jesuit Pass—that links, in the largest vision, the blue Pacific with the goods and markets of the East. Brigham Young was a man of the largest vision. At his behest in 1850, Madison Whickham led a band of the faithful, Latter-day Saints, some two hundred of them, including fifteen slaves, led them over rugged mountains, white deserts, and the canyons of the Colorado River and down to the St. Elmo Valley through Jesuit Pass. Later, in the 1870s, the railroads saw the wisdom of Great Brigham's vision: the blue Pacific linked with the goods and markets of the East through a southerly route. The railroad built its terminus in St. Elmo, crowned in 1898 with that Moorish monstrosity of a station. There, on a still-dark November morning in 1924, a special train— one engine, one passenger car, paid for by St. Elmo National Bank and Trust—chugged and puffed, waiting to collect three passengers. The men took separate seats. They had little to say to one another. They alternately slept and stared silently out their separate windows as the train pulled eastward, up the long grade of Jesuit Pass, to its summit, and thence down through tiny towns, or more correctly collections of dwellings with names attesting to wishful thinking (Pear Valley) or hope and failure (Peru), or names that were simply literal transcriptions of reality, like Jackrabbit Junction. At Jackrabbit Junction, the men switched trains and chugged out the spur line, which, like a tiny black seam stitched across a white desert petticoat, connected Chagrin Springs to Jackrabbit Junction and thus the whole world.

In the middle of the white desert, Chagrin Springs was a small oasis much beloved by the Indians. In 1908, a United States Department of Agriculture agronomist planted Arabian date suckers there, cultivated them, and gave the dozen streets colorful thematic names reminiscent of his travels in North Africa and the Holy Land. Surrounded by acres of date palms, Chagrin Springs huddled around a central core— the springs themselves—like Arabs with their backs to the wind. The county had found it a convenient place for its prison; a prison could look accommodating beside the white waste of desert beyond.

The spur line ended at a date-packing house outside Chagrin Springs proper—if Chagrin Springs could be called proper. There, by prearrangement, Otis, Art, and Lucius were met by a man with a truck. He had been paid to take them to the end of Cairo Street, where Miss Martha Emmons lived with her younger sister, Mrs. Agnes Kreuger, a military widow, both women surviving, just barely, on Agnes's pension and Martha's meager savings.

The driver pulled up before a house that was probably plaster slathered over adobe. It had been painted once but had long since faded. The curtains in the window might once have been a forest green, but they too had faded unto gray. The whole of this hunkered-down dwelling was framed and shaded by magnificent date palms, which stood around it like soldiers from some elite unit guarding a small impoverished country. The truck halted and the driver killed the engine. The three men, none of them spry, alighted clumsily, Lucius and Otis from the truck bed, Art from his uneasy perch beside the driver.

The bleached-out door opened, and a small pale woman with frantic eyes greeted them.

"We have come to see Miss Martha Emmons," announced Otis McGahey with his impossible hauteur. "We wired."

She closed the door. They waited a full fifteen minutes,

and then she returned and bade them step into a small stuffy parlor with the once-green drapes, which were closed. The walls were adorned with outlandish ormolu picture frames encircling hair wreaths and chromos of the real Cairo. Mrs. Kreuger explained she'd been there once with her late husband. Indeed, she might have elaborated, but she was peremptorily hushed and dismissed by a small, sharp-chinned woman with thick white hair pulled taut and high on her head like a pincushion. She sat on one of two mothy horsehair chairs before a low table with bowed legs. The chairs were draped with crocheted antimacassars, the table dotted with doilies yellow with age. Miss Emmons had left St. Elmo clad in brown and she still wore brown. With quick nervous movements, she righted the cameo brooch and the lace at her collar. The lace was soiled in one place where she habitually fretted it.

Otis McGahey introduced his companions and added that they had come all the way from St. Elmo to see her on a matter of the gravest importance.

"Henry," said Miss Emmons, lifting her sharp chin. "Henry's set up at Shiloh, hasn't he? Am I correct?" she added, as though these three men were no more than sniveling schoolboys who had best know their sums.

Lucius stepped forward and assured her she was right.

"How did you know to come here? How did you know about Henry and me?" she demanded.

"Hank Beecham told me some time ago that you and he had married, Miss Emmons," Lucius offered.

"And did Henry tell you I divorced him? Yes, I am a divorced woman!" She flung this at them with the panache of an oath or an expletive, all the more odd coming from so frail and tiny a woman. "A divorcée! The sort of woman your wives would shun in the street. You yourselves would pay me no respectable heed, and yet here you are begging at my feet."

"I wouldn't say that exactly," Otis began.

"I would," Doctor corrected him. "You're absolutely right again, Miss Emmons. We are here to beg."

"*Après moi, le déluge,*" she retorted.

"What?" said Art.

"I don't expect you to remember your history," she said to Art and Otis in such a way as to render them once more in short pants. "I remember you well as philistines and pharisees, so I don't expect that either of *you* would have the least acquaintance with history or literature. But I should think, Doctor Tipton, that you, as a man of breeding and reading and culture, even though you are an atheist, *you* might remember the source and import of that quote."

Reduced to schoolboy stammering, Lucius identified the quote as coming from Louis the Fifteenth and foreshadowing the French Revolution. She seemed satisfied with Doctor's answer. He half-expected her to tell him he could take his seat.

"Miss Emmons," Art began in his best Bank and Trust manner, "we are here to ask you to intervene with your husband on behalf of the—"

"I have no husband! I have told you. I am a divorced woman. I married Henry Beecham in Texas and the eyes of God, and divorced him in the sight of the law. For twelve years, I followed that man from town to town all over the West. For twelve years, I breathed the stink of his sweat and sulphur and dynamite and gunpowder. I held him in my arms, I slept beside him on dirt floors, in sheds with no more than a blanket for a door. I rode on trains from Mexico to Wyoming. I rode in wagons filled with dynamite, explosives, and gunpowder. I followed him to every parched and stinking hole that needed rain, every dried-up ranch and dried-out rancher who believed Henry Beecham could give them what God had refused. I did my duty as a wife. I did everything required of a wife. I suffered as a wife. I—"

"Did you love him?" Lucius asked mildly.

"What?"

"Love him. Did you love him?"

Miss Emmons stroked her collar and then peered from face to face, as though trying to place the names of unruly students. "You're all so old," she said at last. "You're all so wretchedly, horribly old!"

"Miss Emmons," Art Whickham beseeched her, "please—"

"Get out," she snapped. "Do you think for one minute I

care about Henry Beecham? Get out!"

"It's St. Elmo, Miss Emmons," Otis remonstrated.

"That squalid revolting town! How could I care about St. Elmo? I? I despise St. Elmo and everyone in it, as they have despised me. Get out, I say! You're all so old I cannot endure the sight of you. It is immaterial to me what happens to St. Elmo. Let God or Henry wash it out to sea! Get out! Get out!" She rose; she seemed to fly at them with her white hands. "I hate the very sight of you! Agnes!"

As befit the widow of a military man, Agnes Kreuger did just as she was bid, ushering the three men out quickly. She pushed Art Whickham and closed the door behind them. In the shade of the towering palms, they faced each other wordlessly and then started toward the waiting truck.

CHAPTER SEVEN

Otis and I had no sooner hoisted ourselves into the back of the truck, Art snatching the seat beside the driver, when Agnes Kreuger came flying out of the house, arms waving, crying, "Doctor! Doctor! Come quick! It's Martha! She fell down! She's stopped breathing!"

I hastened out of the truck and made for the door. So did Otis and Art, but Agnes barred their way. Once I was inside, she closed that door in their faces, locked it with an affirmative snap, and smiled. "In there." She pointed me back to the parlor, where I found Miss Emmons not at all dying on the floor but sitting perfectly upright in her chair, still fidgeting with the soiled lace on the collar of her brown dress.

She motioned for me to take the other chair. "You have to understand, Doctor, it was not his father who was at fault," she began with no other explanation. "His father was drunk and disgusting, of course, a lout pure and simple, vulgar beyond belief, a man beneath contempt, but he was not at fault. Virginia probably died in a whorehouse having done no one but herself any harm. The one brother—I forget his name—he died in a brawl before he could do any real damage. The other one died in prison. Horace was ever a worthless drunk. Worthless but harmless. But Henry was the worst of the lot. The worst of a rotten family."

Surprised, I stammered, "But Miss Emmons, Hank was the best of that family, not the worst."

"He might have been," she conceded as if considering some point of grammar, "but for his mother. She perverted his every gift. Blame Eulalie. His sainted, long-suffering mother, the brave, stalwart, loving Eulalie Beecham. Blame her for the wreck of a man who holds St. Elmo hostage. It's her fault entirely. Does that shock you, Doctor?"

"I am too old to be shocked," I replied, not quite certain what was under discussion.

"Old! Old!" The word caught in a cackle in her throat. "We're all old, aren't we, Doctor? Old and ugly." She regarded me critically. "But you weren't always so, Doctor. No, indeed, I remember you as quite attractive. I remember a time when, if you had not been an atheist, if you had converted to Mormonism or Methodism or showed any inclination to embrace convention, you would have been besieged with young women wanting to marry you."

"I was spared that."

"You never married, then?"

"No."

"Humph. Then it was unmitigated gall on your part to ask me if I loved my husband."

"Forgive me, Miss Emmons, but this is an emergency and I am too old to be delicate."

"I was born old, Doctor. Wouldn't you agree?"

"Why are you begging me to insult you, Miss Emmons?"

"Insult is nothing to me, Doctor. A born-old spinster who teaches stupid children in a scabby railroad town grows absolutely immune to insult. Insult is nothing to me." She quit fidgeting with her collar and applied her hands to a shiny spot on her brown skirt. "Of course, you can understand why I left St. Elmo without a word. I was not about to have insult heaped upon my marriage. Not as insult had been heaped upon my spinsterhood. I was not about to have the very flies over my head buzz and whisper, *The besotted old virgin Martha Emmons, she's marrying a boy from the lowest white family in town. She's throwing away her refinements and education to marry an ignorant boy fifteen years younger than she. A woman with a certificate from Spartana Normal School is marrying a boy who fixes sewing machines, just to have a Mrs. before her name and a man in her bed. She'd marry a goat if it walked upright. She'd—"*

"Miss Emmons, I don't think you're—"

"Don't think, Doctor! Above all, do not tell me I am wrong! Please. Do not tell me that you place great faith in the charitable instincts of St. Elmo."

"St. Elmo is a place like any other, Miss Emmons. Sometimes, you have to extend tolerance even when you don't find charity." I fidgeted. Maybe it was just the horsehair in the chair, but I had the feeling that I was in an audience, one of many watching while she declaimed on some gaslit stage.

"Such insult was intolerable to me. I well knew what St. Elmo thought of me. A spinster is a figure of ridicule and condescension. The most lowly groveling cur of a woman, like Eulalie Beecham, a bitch"—she spat the odd phrase tartly—"could look down on me, a woman of learning and refinement, a woman with a certificate from Spartana Normal School, simply because Eulalie was married and I was not. Indeed, such is the weight of convention that I might have been tempted to trade my education, my expectations, everything I'd earned in life—and I assure you I did earn it, Doctor; nothing was given Martha Emmons!—in order to be married. Such is the dreary unenviable lot of the spinster. Many's the teacher who has forsworn her independence for the sake of propriety. Many's the woman who has cast off her education to give herself in marriage to some loveless brute merely for the sake of being wed. I might have been tempted to such an ignoble life, but I chose against it. I had always vowed that love alone, Doctor, love alone would unite me to a man. Without love, I would not have forsaken my independence. I would have endured—endlessly—the snickers of stupid boys, the guffaws of bovine girls, the sniveling sanctimony of women like Sister Whitworth and Eulalie Beecham. Because without love, Doctor, what is the point? Mere stultifying convention. Without love—I ask you—what profiteth it?"

I don't believe I had ever heard that old biblical injunction (usually trotted out to excuse greed) put to such poetic use. I was moved. Hank Beecham was altogether right, Martha Emmons could certainly give you a fine talk-to.

"But the truth of it is, Doctor, in answer to your question, I loved Henry Beecham. I never intended to love him, but I did. I fell in love. We were both in love, in the grip of a forbidden passion. The difference in our ages was but a cruel trick of nature. Our souls were plighted, whatever the difference in our ages and circumstances."

Her pinched pale face softened with an endearing charm, and though I could not quite picture her young, I could imagine her in love.

"I wrestled mightily with guilt for loving Henry. I vowed nightly to renounce him. Each night, I would pray beside my bed in Sister Whitworth's boardinghouse, on my knees I' I'd beg God to deliver me from loving a man that much younger, that much my social inferior, my inferior in every way, a low ignorant boy who fixes sewing machines and worships his sainted mother. And then, when I was done praying, I would get up from my knees and look in the bit of mirror over the washstand and smile just to think of his sweetness, to think how his blue eyes would light to look on me, how he blossomed in my company and I in his. We illuminated one another, I tell you. We enhanced one another. I loved his thirst for knowledge, his hunger for achievement, his ambition. I loved him for his passion. I knew I would love him till the day I died." Miss Emmons ran her fingers along her cheek, slowly stroking, then brought both hands to rest firmly in her lap and regarded me with an unendurable honesty. "I loved him to Distraction."

She said this last like a knowable place, a geographical entity that I, as a student, ought to be able to point to on a map. I did not contradict or question her, but I was certainly bewildered. I asked if she would mind if I smoked my cigar. It was a terrible thing to ask an old lady, but I was desperate.

"Not at all," she said to my surprise. "Agnes!" When Agnes appeared, Martha commanded her to bring a china saucer for my ashes. She came quickly back with the saucer, which had a faded gay rosebud print round the rim. "She is a good girl," Martha said of her sister when she had left the room. "Reliable."

"I could have guessed as much."

"Could you have guessed, Doctor, that Henry Beecham and I were lovers before we ever were man and wife?" Miss Emmons said this with such obvious reckless pride that I feigned shock. "Yes. Well, we were," she added smugly. "Our love of learning flowed into a much fuller and deeper love. Love in the flesh and in the spirit. I loved him to Distraction," she repeated.

I needed the cigar. It cleared my head, if not this airless ancient parlor. As I listened to her, I began to recognize the curious quality of her speech. It owed its flavor to old-fashioned novels, probably to hundreds and hundreds of forgettable novels, books Miss Emmons had read over the years, books written by women authors who turned out thousands of them, no doubt to support households of greedy brats left them by feckless husbands. Dusty novels, musty, redolent of virtue rewarded and love fulfilled, plighted troths, renunciations, reunions, novels where sturdy young men fell in love with dainty heroines, enslaved by these girls' uplifted lips and downcast eyes. Miss Emmons must have envisioned herself in that role time and time again, must have seen the lanky taciturn Hank as the hero. I smoked, listened attentively, nodded, all the while trying to peel back the veneer of time so clearly cracking on both Miss Emmons and Hank Beecham, to imagine them as they must have seemed to one another. And it was not hard to imagine an ignorant brutalized boy. Hank grew up dodging the belt and the fist, flinched every time he heard his father's hand crack across his mother's face, wept every time Eulalie screamed, or cried out, or begged not to be beaten, and Hank winced every time he heard his father's lust grunt over his sister's body. And Virginia? Did she cry out? Or was she silent? And was that silence by far more terrible? This boy had only just escaped all that, rescued himself and his mother from all that misery. This boy wanted more than escape, though. He dreamed of rain, rain created from the soggy rage of a pitiless drunk. And then this boy is offered the friendship and admiration of a learned woman who actually believes in his dreams, believes in his capacity to make rain, to make science, possibly to make history. She gives him her time, her guidance, her didactic skills. Then her love. Her body. She marries him, follows him all over the West.

I watched Miss Emmons fretting her collar, speaking in phrases borrowed from books where virtue and passion and courage were rewarded as they had never been in her own life. But even if she borrowed the phrases from books, her own passion and courage were not borrowed. Those were truly hers. And she had thrown all of this into the education of a boy who had actually challenged her with something more than dirty words scrawled on the board behind her back. A boy (perhaps the first person ever) who wanted what Martha Emmons had to give. Hank Beecham must have waked in her some tender confusion that could not be assuaged by stale phrases, nor denied on behalf of the conventions which had shackled Miss Emmons all her life. When she met Hank, she was old enough to be fettered to the conventions of spinsterhood, but was courageous enough to defy them. It came to me, listening, that the truly reckless thing Miss Emmons had done was not in bedding down with Hank before marriage, but in having the courage to love him at all. A lesser woman would have faltered, turned away, comforted herself with cold rectitude and martyred renunciation. In the back of my mind, I heard the spindly strains of "Believe Me, If All Those Endearing Young Charms" in a sort of duet with "The Last Rose of Summer," as she perched before me on the horsehair chair smoothing an imaginary wrinkle from her brown dress.

I dribbled ashes into the saucer, and when she paused in her old-fashioned narrative, I tried to steer back to my original purpose. "Miss Emmons, I believe you loved him. I believe that. But I must tell you what I don't believe. I don't believe it was the rainmaker's life, the stink and the squalor, that made you leave him."

"It might have been different if we'd had children."

Reflecting that those were Hank Beecham's words in 1916, I winced for the loss they implied.

"But we didn't," she went on, her fingers back to fondling her collar. "However, it wasn't the rainmaker's life that drove me to leave him. I hated him."

"To Distraction?"

"No," Miss Emmons supplied in a corrective voice. "I *loved* him to Distraction. I hated him because he didn't love me."

"Oh, I don't think that's true."

"He didn't, I tell you. I lived with him, and the more I loved him, the more I hated him. I have never quit loving him, and I have never quit hating him. It's never changed. The years have not acted as a palliative for Henry. Why should they for me? Do you understand?"

"Hank says time means nothing to him."

"Humph. You do not understand." She combined schoolmarm smugness with a duchess's declamation. "They are not mutually exclusive, hate and love, even though we're told they are. They are not like Newtonian physics, where no two particles may inhabit the same space at the same time."

"The heart won't always follow the laws of physics."

"The heart is unreliable at best."

"But it's all we have," I insisted. "All you have. You and Hank."

"Agnes!" Miss Emmons shouted. When Mrs. Kreuger's head rounded the door, Miss Emmons said, "I'm sure the doctor has had a fatiguing journey. Would you like a cup of tea and a bite to eat, Doctor?"

"What about the others, Martha?" Agnes nodded toward the front window. "One of them says he has to, you know . . .

Shall I let him use the commode?"

"Most certainly not! Let him urinate in the desert."

"Shall I feed the others, Martha?"

Miss Emmons paused. "Isn't there some mush left over from breakfast, Agnes? Oatmeal mush?"

"Some."

"Very well. Feed them mush."

"Shall I sugar it, Martha?"

"No sugar, no milk, no cream," replied Miss Emmons. "It will do those men good to eat unleavened mush. Of course, first you'll want to see to Doctor's ham and biscuits. The biscuits are fresh, Doctor. Agnes does a very nice biscuit."

I thanked Mrs. Kreuger, and when she left us, I shifted in my chair and began again. "If you still love Hank, Miss Emmons, won't you please come back with me and go to Shiloh to talk to him? I believe you can dissuade him."

"Oh, you truly don't understand! It's more complicated than that. I? I rouse Henry from some course of action on which he has already set his will?"

"But maybe not his heart, Miss Emmons. Maybe he hasn't set his heart to it yet."

"How could I go to a man whom I divorced before all the world and ask anything of him? It was, it will always be, forever final."

"We're not talking about the divorce, Miss Emmons. Love does not always follow legal decrees. Love is like rain. Sometimes, you can bar your door against it and still find your feet wet the next morning. What does it matter if you divorced before the world if you loved him in your heart?"

"I hated him," she reminded me with a verbal rap on the knuckles.

"He never quit loving you, Miss Emmons. He said *I Do*, and no judge could ever change that for him. That's what he told me. He told me that would never change. And what's more, Miss Emmons, I think you never quit loving him either. I think you love Henry Beecham still."

For a moment, she seemed off balance, as though the Sir Walter Scott phrases she habitually used refused to come to her aid.

"Please come back to St. Elmo with me, Miss Emmons. Even if Hank has set himself on this terrible course of action, we have to try to save him. It behooves us to try," I threw in, hoping the phrase might appeal to her novelistic notions.

After fretting her collar, she put her hands in her lap. "Try, if you must. But do not ask me to be party to any undertaking in which Eulalie Beecham has the slightest role. She came between us, the viper. She told Henry his affection for me was killing her. Really, that foul creature, she told him that in loving me, he was killing her. She said low things about me to Henry. She said I was deflecting him from his purpose. It hurt him. You can't imagine how it hurt him."

"She certainly hurt you. It was a disservice to you," I said, flattering shamelessly.

"Henry was absolutely loyal to her, and I never knew until later the things she'd said about me, the vile things. She hurt Henry, cut him to the quick, but every night, he went home to her. Henry adored her."

"Well," I offered, "she didn't deflect him from marrying you, did she?"

"She came between us," Miss Emmons declared again, like I'd missed the point. "She came between us while she lived, and she came between us from the grave. Her teachings. Her teachings had Henry all curdled and soured. I spent twelve years trying to unlearn him, Doctor! Me! A teacher! A certificate from Spartana Normal School! I tried for twelve years to unlearn that man everything he'd imbibed at his mother's knee."

I remonstrated, "What could a woman as beaten and broken as Eulalie Beecham ever have taught him that could be that destructive? I don't believe it."

"*Never forget*," said Miss Emmons succinctly, and the phrase echoed in my mind like a pebble falling down a well. "Henry could not love me because he was so busy doing her bidding, doing everything Eulalie said. *Never forget*. That woman blighted him." Miss Emmons's upper lip curled. "Whatever prospects or possibilities for love Henry had, Eulalie snatched them from him. If she had died while he was still a child, Henry Beecham might have been a whole man."

I was thoughtful at this, but I still pointed out the obvious. "Eulalie Beecham protected Hank and Virginia as best she could. Eulalie Beecham tried to spare them Jeremiah's wrath."

"Eulalie Beecham ruined his life," Miss Emmons insisted. "His noble, long-suffering, sainted mother. She perverted Henry's intelligence. She taught him all too well." Miss Emmons successfully fought tears, but her shoulders rolled forward and her prim lips quivered. "She taught him how to hate. *Never forget*, not a slight, not a debt, not a defeat, not a shame—of which she had many. She taught him all that before I taught him anything."

"I think you endow her with more passion than she ever had, Miss Emmons. She was a hard woman with nothing much to live for, except Hank."

"And she made him live for her, don't you see? He was to avenge Eulalie Beecham for everything she could not forget and was too puny and powerless and weak to do for herself. Henry thought she was a tower of strength. I tell you, Doctor, she was a tower of weakness! She educated—yes, yes, it *is* the correct word!—she educated him to avenge her for the invention of corn whiskey, for drought and locusts, for windgall in horses and foot rot in sheep, cholera in hogs and ticks on chickens. For marrying a drunk and bearing louts and whores, bringing them forth in pain and watching them die drunk and in prison. Henry was to avenge her for everything, beginning with Grant at Shiloh, for the triumph of the Union army and the death of Patrick Cleburne, for Cleburne's stupid, inglorious, inconsequential death at the Battle of Franklin! Have you ever heard of such a battle, Doctor?"

I said I had not.

"No one has! Everyone knows of Shiloh, don't they? But no one's ever heard of Franklin. And do you know why, Doctor? Do you know why Jeremiah Beecham and people like him wail and blubber and bemoan Shiloh? Because at Shiloh, things might have changed. The end might have been different. But by Franklin, the end was foreordained. Franklin was nothing but a mass suicide. November 1864. Sixty years ago. Almost to the day," she added, her schoolmarm's reflexes kicking in. "Under orders and for a mile and a half of open ground under withering fire, Cleburne's troops charged, and when they got to the Federal lines, they fought hand to hand, and those who weren't bayoneted were taken prisoner, and the rest of them lay dead, filling up a ten-foot trench in front of the Federal defenses. And for nothing! They attacked for nothing! Cleburne was one of the six Confederate generals who died that day, Doctor. Six generals! All those men knew they had lost the War and hadn't the courage to face the peace. How much easier is it to go out in a blaze of

smoke and glory? A single merciful bullet through the heart."
Miss Emmons's voice shook, and she trembled visibly, though
with which emotions I could not tell. "When they found
Cleburne's body, his boots had been stolen. By one of his
own."

"That's not uncommon in warfare," I said, in defense of I
didn't know who.

"Jeremiah Beecham wanted to die at Franklin too, and
yet he was one of those few God chose to live. How could
God be so crass? So futile? Show such Almighty bad taste?
Patrick Cleburne dies and Jeremiah Beecham comes marching home to the girl he left behind? Jeremiah lives so he can
desert the rest of the War and desert the peace too? So he
can drag Eulalie and her brats out here to California, desert
the living, and lie dead drunk in his own vomit? He beat
Eulalie senseless with the Bonnie Blue Flag, beat his sons too.
The sons drank so they could forget battles they'd never even
fought. Her only daughter, a thief, ran off in the night. Oh,
Eulalie Beecham had a lot to forget or avenge." Miss Emmons
snorted. "You can see which path she chose."

"It might not have been noble, but it's surely understand-
able," I volunteered, thinking it was altogether understand-
able even without knowing the truth of Virginia Beecham's
flight, a fact which clearly Hank had never parted with, even
to his wife.

"Eulalie insisted, instilled in Henry, schooled him, taught

him to make it all up to her, because she could never forget. And she never did. The purposes, Doctor . . ." Miss Emmons took deep desperate breaths. "The purposes she thought I might deflect him from had nothing to do with his, his . . ."

"Dreams? His dreams?" I supplied like oxygen.

"Nothing to do with his dreams. Yes." Miss Emmons frantically ran both hands over her skirt, smoothing it till at last she caught her breath and could continue. "I am not without my charitable instincts, but they would be utterly squandered on Eulalie Beecham, dead or alive."

I put my cigar out in the saucer, ashamed of having smoked it at all. A man could maybe smoke around a New Woman, but in this parlor and with this passionate relic, it seemed a lapse of manners on my part. Having collected herself, Martha Emmons softened, even her little sharp chin softening. She said that in their years together, she alone could make Henry Beecham smile, even laugh. "It's difficult to imagine him laughing," I admitted.

"You see, Doctor, love alone might have saved him. Love alone." She ruminated over the phrase. "Love alone might have deflected him from carrying out all Eulalie's wrath and anger and hate and hurt. And I loved him. My courage, my tenacity were equal to that love. But I knew, finally . . . Well, Doctor, I asked only to be loved in return. That isn't so much, is it?"

"One wouldn't think so, Miss Emmons."

"After twelve years of marriage, I knew I would always be defeated, that my voice, my tenderness, my appeal would make no inroad on his heart. I had been vanquished by his insufferable mother. Eulalie used his quick mind—he was quite the most brilliant student, I say that without the complications of love—to soak up all the hate and remembrance she could give him. Eulalie was nasty and low minded, a she-serpent. *Never forget,*" Miss Emmons all but spit.

I tried to picture Eulalie Beecham as a she-serpent but could recall only a woman who mopped up the mess her daughter had made of her innards without a flicker of judgment or, for that matter (I had to admit), a flicker of tenderness or even compassion. Eulalie Beecham was as efficient in her care of Virginia as she might have been with a ewe or a sow. At the time, I thought she was humiliated to have called a doctor out to Shiloh to tend a self-inflicted abortion on an unmarried girl. But perhaps that was my own sense of convention. Now, knowing what I knew of Virginia Beecham, what her mother knew as well, I wondered, all these years later, I questioned Eulalie saying to me, *I'll never forget this, Doctor. Never.* I heard Hank's voice too, spiraling over Eulalie's, *You'll never forget this, Doctor. Never.*

Agnes brought in a chipped tin tray with a chipped earthenware teapot, two saucerless cups, and an enameled plate of a half-dozen still-warm biscuits and (I reckoned) their whole week's ration of ham. Miss Emmons passed me the plate.

"Thank you, Miss Emmons, but I'm not very hungry."

"Please do not do me the gross injustice of lying, Doctor Tipton. It doth not become you." She handed me a cup of tea. "Don't worry about your friends. Agnes does a quite nice oatmeal mush."

"They're not my friends, Miss Emmons. I have no connection with them except that we are all equally concerned about the valley, about what Hank Beecham intends to do to St. Elmo, and we're here to ask you to—"

"Eat your ham and biscuits, Doctor Tipton. I shall not be rushed. You owe me the deference of an older person. I am older than you, aren't I?"

I took a bite to avoid replying.

"I could not teach Henry to love. That she-serpent had got to him first. I was defeated from the beginning. Time is the great palliative, Doctor. Time is mercy. Those who are denied the mercy of time live in a kind of hell, a kind of perdition. Eulalie denied Henry the mercies of time. If Henry has a quarrel with St. Elmo, he will never forget it. He doesn't think there is a past, don't you understand? It's all Eulalie's fault," she added petulantly. "His not loving me, that was all Eulalie's fault too."

"And because you are of a tidy cast of mind, you decided to divorce him and be done with it. Forever final?"

"Exactly. I wanted nothing left undone, no possibility of reunion to taunt or tempt or torture me, so I decided to endure the public infamy of divorce and be done with it."

"But you weren't done with him, Miss Emmons. It wasn't forever final. You let him pay off Shiloh through your Paydirt bank."

Like a teacher who has been asked a question she cannot answer, Miss Emmons took refuge in the oblique. "I shall never speak to Henry Beecham again. I would not ask that man to pass me the salt," she concluded triumphantly.

"And yet, Miss Emmons, he asked a good deal more than the salt of you. He asked you to be party to a hoax which you knew, you must have known, could only be done in the name of revenge."

"He did not ask me," she maintained stiffly. "He wrote me a letter."

"Did you know about the 1917 flood?"

Miss Emmons creaked out a squeaky laugh that sounded like an inexperienced fiddler trying out a new bow. "What does 1917 matter? I told you. He's avenging something quite apart from time or money."

But I went pointedly on, determined to lay out the unpolished facts. "He made a bet for fifty thousand dollars with those men eating mush outside. Hank brought the rain and filled the reservoir, but the dam broke. There was a lot of damage. They refused to pay him, and he vowed to avenge himself on the town. He's out there now, at Shiloh, which you paid off—"

"Not I. He sent the money. I sent the draft."

"Why? Why?" I demanded, insisted. "You divorced him. You say you hated him. He broke your heart. Why did you help him then? Why won't you help him now?"

"If Henry vowed he'd come back and blow you all up, wash you out to sea, or rain St. Elmo to oblivion, I'm very sorry, Doctor, but there's nothing I can do to help you. Henry was always very faithful."

"And you, Miss Emmons, are you faithful? Hank told me you were always making vows, vowing this and that, swearing fealty, love, honor, for better or for worse."

"I divorced him so as to have it be forever final."

"If it was not final then, if you broke that vow and made the payments from your bank, then please, Miss Emmons, let it not be forever final now. Help me. Come with me to Shiloh. See him again. Help him. Help me. Undo Eulalie's work."

"Send in the army. It will take an army to stop Henry. Only an army can undo Eulalie's work."

I was going to protest and argue, to thump and storm, but I kept thinking about Patrick Cleburne, about Shiloh and Franklin. Maybe that was my situation. Maybe I should have done more to stop Hank in 1917, but by 1924, maybe it was all foreordained, like Franklin. "He'll die out there, Miss Emmons. You know as well as I do that's what he intends. It's a suicide, though it is to look like a battle. Like Franklin.

Hank will die, and there may be also a lot of pain and damage inflicted on innocent people in St. Elmo."

She gave a withering sniff and snapped at me, "I despise St. Elmo."

I stood up. "If you won't help me, then I can't waste any more time here, because time does mean something to me. But I have to tell you, Miss Emmons, that the viciousness that you hate in Eulalie Beecham, you've got it. You've got it just as surely as if it were a bacillus you'd shared in drinking from her same cup. If she passed it on to Hank, she passed it on to you too."

"You don't understand."

"Oh, yes. Yes, I do. You did not love him to Distraction, Miss Emmons. And for a woman so broadly fond of vows, you have broken the very ones he has kept. You were not equal to Hank, Miss Emmons. And you are no better than Eulalie. You say love alone could have saved him from Eulalie, but you are not willing to try."

"Twelve years! Twelve years I tried."

"That was the past. This is the present."

"Time means nothing to Henry."

"Well, then you have truly drunk from Eulalie Beecham's cup, Miss Emmons. You are using Hank for your own purposes, just like she did. You want him to avenge you. You want him to avenge all the wrongs you suffered as a spinster. You have contributed to this battle, Miss Emmons, and by God I believe you ought to take some responsibility!"

"I can't help you."

"You won't help me."

"I won't help you," she repeated, as if it were the dates of the Punic Wars.

I left her there in her cramped airless parlor still stroking the soiled lace of her collar, much as she must have stroked her own cheek those nights of her lonely virginity when she went to the mirror above the washstand and smiled to think of Henry Beecham, to dream of loving him to Distraction and Texas, to Arizona and Nevada, to Sonora and Chihuahua and all the dry, dry places in between.

The door flew open and Hank burst out, rifle poised in his arms, sights leveled on me. "Don't come no further. Don't come one inch or I blow you straight to hell! This minute's your last on earth."

"It's me! Lucius Tipton. I'm alone."

"I don't give a damn. There's nothing I want to say, nothing I want to hear. I'll never surrender. I'll never retreat. Step foot on my property and you're a dead man."

Nonetheless, in a calculated act, I did step out of the Ford, waved my white flag, which was tied to a stick. I choked, and my eyes stung in the cruel carboniferous air, granulated with ash and cinders and smoke. The cauldrons yet burned, but I could not tell if the incendiary fan had yet been laid.

Squinting into the dusky light, though, I noticed that the shack seemed to have sprouted a queer little picket fence, tiny white pickets lined up like little sentries. No curtains at the windows. No flowers by the door. Rockets. Waving the white flag in an arc, I took a step forward. A bullet whistled past, so close that I felt its draft. "You already won, Hank. You struck the fear of God into St. Elmo."

"I don't give a damn about God."

"People are on your side. There's been a fearful outcry against Art and them. Sid's left town. You won the bet. Everyone wants to see you get your money."

"I don't need the money."

"And St. Elmo doesn't need the rain. People want to see you get what you deserve and Eulalie get her marble angel. They've taken up a subscription, Hank. They want to make it up to you, what she suffered. The battle is over."

"The hell you say. Talk's finished. Leave, Doctor."

"You might be General Cleburne, Hank, you might be at that, but it's Franklin you're fighting. You know that battle, Hank?" He remained where he was, rifle beaded on me, and nodded without speaking. "Are you going to die like that? It amounted to suicide. At least Patrick Cleburne believed in something, died for something he believed in. Where's your glorious cause? It was a bet. That's all. A preposterous bet, and you won. You already said it's not the money. So what is it? Dying out here on account of a curse? Who was cursed,

Hank? You sure it was St. Elmo? You sure it wasn't your own family?" I went on, more of the same, as long as he'd let me talk, skirting but never directly stating what Miss Emmons had told me of Eulalie Beecham. And in truth, to think of the long-suffering Eulalie Beecham as a vessel of wrath was something I could hardly get my mind around. The thought shocked me, like Hank had been shocked years ago when I'd pointed out that his father had looted the sword, buttons, and epaulettes off a dead man, that they hadn't been taken in the thick of battle. "Are you killing yourself for Eulalie, Hank? Well, that's a real victory for her. Is that what she wanted?"

"I'm telling you for the last time, Doctor. Leave. You know my position here."

"Let the battle be over. You've won. Victory." I started to move closer, but a bullet screamed past. I dropped the white flag in the dust. "So be it. If you don't put out those fires, they're coming out here to kill you. They're bringing the army."

From the shack came the tactical question, "When?"

In fact, I didn't know when. Didn't know for a fact that the army would attack. Knew only what the rest of St. Elmo knew, that the sheriff was beseeching the United States Army to relieve him of this responsibility. If I'd known the time of the attack, I would have told Hank, I suppose. I suppose that's part of the trust I'd struck with him, but I had not the stomach for it. As a doctor, it's my sworn duty to struggle with death, not to embrace it. I don't believe in glorious death, in battle or anywhere else. I believe that death alone is forever final. And I am on the side of life, of life's processes, however imperfect and unlovely.

"You delivered your message, Doctor. You better git."

"I got one more message, Hank. I talked to Martha. I have a message from Martha. I saw her this afternoon." I waited, hoping he'd answer. But he didn't, so I went on. "I just got back. She's not living in Paydirt anymore. She's here, here in this county. She's living down in the desert at Chagrin Springs with her sister."

After a long silence, he asked, "Which one?"

"Agnes. Martha's been there since 1921."

"What's the message?"

"It was not forever final, the divorce. She still loves you." This was not what she had said, of course, but I believed it was what she meant, and even if she hadn't, and even if she'd refused to come in person to help me save Hank, I was not above enlisting her aid. "She has always loved you. She will always love you. Time means nothing to her, and nothing can change her love for you." I aimed the words carefully into the darkness at a man I could see only as shadow. "You still have a chance. You and Martha." And this I thought might be true.

Hank fired again. This bullet struck the earth not far from

the Ford. So I had my answer. I took a deep defeated breath. "Do you have some last message? For her? For anyone?"

"No message. No mercy. No retreat. No surrender. Fire and rain! Victory!"

A match flickered, and I could see him bend, without haste or grandeur, to the white picket fence he'd built before Shiloh's tumble-down shack. One by one, the white-capped, handmade rockets shot into the air, wheezing, whinnying their high whistles, their bright flares blazing into the night as I got back in the Ford, turned around, and left Shiloh behind me.

CHAPTER NINE

Two days later (December 1, 1924, at 3:10 P.M., according to my pocket watch), blasts shook the St. Elmo Valley one after another. Blanche fell over, books rained from my shelves, bottles crashed in the surgery, where I was tending little Nanette Bowers, who screamed. Her mother screamed too, and they both dove under the table in the surgery, crying out, "Earthquake! Earthquake!" Even though I could feel the house shudder, the thunder and rumble in the earth, I knew it wasn't an earthquake. Hank Beecham had ended the war. Perhaps it felt like victory to him. It did not feel so to me. Tears started in my eyes.

Maybe I was the only one in St. Elmo who knew what had happened. Everyone else in this town, they've been waiting for the army to make their move. But the army hadn't. The sheriff had done his damnedest to convince the army it was a military situation and they should go out there, lay siege to Hank Beecham, fight it out at Shiloh. And basically, the army told the sheriff it was his duty to keep the peace, to restore order. But the sheriff could not have done it, restored order or peace. It was beyond him. Even the army could not have done it. *No message. No mercy. No retreat. No surrender.* Everyone else might believe these blasts unprovoked, but I had seen Hank Beecham, and I knew he did not require an attack, did not need the army to make him aim the Enfield into the shed and pull the trigger, to die where he stood. It was not, after all, a willingness to die where he stood, but an insistence. He had cursed St. Elmo and doomed himself.

I told Mrs. Bowers to keep Nanette safely under the table till it was safe, and I took my hat and left, drove downtown. All the town registered these intermittent blasts as a man might some deep and painful punches. The big new sign in front of St. Elmo High fell forward like an uncaring drunk, and the smart new marquee atop the Dream Theatre dropped off. Colored glass and plaster lay there in the street. The pole in front of Bowers' Barber Shop had fallen over and rolled some distance, though Grief's front window stood.

Many did not. Window glass lay everywhere shining, shattered on the sidewalks, and there were people streaming out of every door from Art's bank to the Chinese laundry, some hollering, some dazed, some grim. There was another blast and rumble, and the cross atop the Baptist chapel teetered and fell. People in the street sat right down where they were, clutching one another, crying out, "He is come! He is come!" I nearly drove over a couple of these fools, swerved to avoid them. I yelled at them to get up, get out of the road, but they continued to clutch and wail, their eyes popping, bulging like they were seeing imps dance in the streets of St. Elmo. And all this as a cloud of smoke the size of Africa began to roll overhead.

At the Pilgrim, I found the front glass shattered, and I dashed inside. Ruth was already cleaning up the mess, some plaster fallen from the ceiling, a few plates and cups in shards. She pressed the broom handle to the white apron at her breast, but her eyes were calm. "That was it, wasn't it?" she asked. "Hank Beecham is dead."

And I said yes, that was it. Forever final.

I got back in the Ford and drove over to the sheriff's, on my way passing by a power pole that had crashed down, landed on top of an ice truck, while the fallen wires protested and sparked in the street and people jumped and shrieked too near them. The church bell at Assumption was tolling, just in case someone in town hadn't noticed the emergency. By the time I got to the sheriff's office, most everyone was already gone, but Floyd and Al were there, just strapping on their guns, checking their rifles and their shells, grabbing up boxes of ammunition.

"You won't need weapons," I said. "You won't need any of that. He's not alive."

"I hope he's not, Doctor, but I am not going anywhere near Shiloh unarmed," returned Floyd.

"You want to prevent deaths, you should get someone over to that power pole that's fallen down on Brigham."

"Let the fire boys do that." But he rang up the operator just the same, told her about the fallen power pole and to get the message to the fire boys. Then he turned to me. "You coming, Doctor?"

"You won't need a doctor. You'll need the coroner, but he's an elected fool."

We took my Ford and headed out toward Shiloh. The cloud of smoke was thicker, denser, closer to earth as we drew nearer. We could hardly breathe, held handkerchiefs over our mouths, and presently we see headlamps and the sheriff's whole regiment coming at us. The sheriff himself pulls his car over beside us, orders us to follow everyone to town, says none of them can go any farther. The smoke, the flames, they're all too terrible.

"There's nothing out at Shiloh," says the sheriff, "but hell and damnation. Flames."

We were still a ways from Shiloh and could not see the actual flames, but the smoke was so thick it reached its talons up around your throat and throttled you, gouged at your eyes, and the fire we could not see could have choked us to death right there. I swung the Ford around and followed the rest of the cars back toward town.

"I guess we'll march on Shiloh when the fire burns itself out," says Al. "It'll burn itself out at Shiloh."

We all three bounce as I hit a rock or the body of an animal in the road. The smoke had clutched its sooty paws to the window, and everything was obscured.

"There's groves on either side of Shiloh," says Floyd after a bit. "Doradel groves. They'll burn. They'll go first."

They don't speak again, neither Al nor Floyd. So I have to say it: "If the wind comes up, if the wind picks up those flames burning at Shiloh, they will go with the wind. Wherever it goes. And if it goes north, it will burn out the railroad bridge. And if it comes south, this whole town will be a fireball, an inferno, and there will be no stopping it."

We watched and we waited to see which way the wind would go. How would the fire burn? Led by the advancing wind, it continued south toward town. Businesses closed down and people stayed close by their homes (buckets lined up on every porch) to see if the wind would bring this brimstone hell, this fiery furnace to St. Elmo. Even the railroad, though it didn't shut down, had to slow. Men were brought in from Los Angeles to work our railroad yards, because all St. Elmo was out on the front lines, fighting the advancing fire. We set up bivouacs at strategic points between the city and the fire, and every able-bodied man in the St. Elmo Valley volunteered, men whose forebears had been brought under the whip and the cross by the Spanish, men whose forebears had fought and bought and cheated the Mexicans out of this land, men like Grief Bowers whose people had been brought to this valley as slaves, Chinese men whose fathers had been imported in human hogsheads to serve the railroad, Mormon men, Gentile and Jewish men, railroad men, cattlemen, farmers, bank tellers, merchants and mechanics, growers and packers and pickers alike. Volunteers all, forged with a single purpose: to fight this fire. We fought together to save what we valued. We should have taken this moment, distilled it, saved it, built on it toward a future when we could be united without a common enemy, without an enemy at all.

But now the fire was our enemy, and we lived and ate and slept as best we could side by side, food, blankets, medical supplies fetched in, the wounded and exhausted fetched back out by a fleet of cars and delivery trucks, Ruth Douglass herself driving the Pilgrim's back and forth, tirelessly ferrying men, supplies, food. I left hospital work to other doctors and remained myself at the front line to work with those emergencies that could not wait to be evacuated. The wind came south and never changed direction and pushed the blaze and smoke before it like a fiery broom, sweeping everything on the east and west flanks. Even as we retreated closer to the city, we had to thank Art Whickham and his goddamn irrigation, because we had a source of water in those goddamn irrigation mains, and even if the fire drank up every drop of water in the earth's crust, we fought that fire with the wells, the artesian wells that were beneath this valley the whole time.

The wind toyed with us, doing a coy destructive dance, blazing up, faltering back, but it did not, would not, never did change direction. As I worked on men suffering terrible burns, inhaled smoke, sleepless exhaustion (their faces, their gums, their mouths, and their nasal passages coated with soot, their hands burned, their hearts breaking), I kept thinking of Grant. How he had pushed back up against the Tennessee River but never crossed it. He retreated before the enemy but had not lost the battle. On the second day, Grant attacked, used his reinforcements to gain ground, to force the Confederates back retreating over that already bloodied ground. I kept telling myself, *Like Grant, we're going to whip this fire yet, and we're going to win even though it looks like all we have is lost.* I said it like a prayer, though I don't believe in praying.

The fire raged forward, burning the groves and everything in its path. For two days, we made stand after stand against the fire, and then the wind died down. The wind died down, then died. Like Grant, we defeated the fire that would have destroyed us. And no man amongst us died.

I had to remind people that no one died. Afterwards, I worked amongst the still-suffering and wounded, and people were bitter and angry with me, knowing I had befriended Hank Beecham. Even as I treated them, they cursed him, muttered at me. Even as I cared for them, they called me a traitor to my own town.

Every church in this city had a day of prayer and thanksgiving after the fire, but there was not one word of mercy for the soul of Hank Beecham. And he himself had said, *No mercy*, hadn't he? Well, he got none. There was no mercy for Hank, who was beyond mercy in any event, beyond suffering, but not beyond mourning. I mourned him. I did not defend what he'd done, but I mourned his death. It seemed to me an unnecessary death. Like Cleburne at the Battle of Franklin, the suicide battle. I thought of Hank like Patrick Cleburne, a brave man gone down before forces which, once set in motion, he could not control. I said so in the note I wrote to Miss Emmons. I felt obliged to write her, though no doubt she read the papers. It was a plain note, and I kept it measured, without blame or censure. My God, hadn't there been enough blame and censure? I was sick of it. All of it. I wanted only the comfort of Ruth's arms, to lay my head on her breast and breathe what did not smell of smoke.

Soon as it was possible, the first morning they could, the sheriff's men, fire officials, they all moved in on Shiloh. I did not go. I came to Bowers' Barber Shop around noon or so, and there was already a group of men gathered waiting for Floyd and Al.

When Floyd and Al arrived, their faces were bleak, smoke streaked. They go straight to the sinks and stick their heads under the taps and come up dripping. Grief himself uncorks a bottle of Majic Bitters Tonic for each deputy. "There isn't much to tell," they say. The fire had burnt up everything in its path, the Doradel groves, all gone. Everything.

"And Shiloh?" I ask. "What did you find there?"

Floyd and Al said Shiloh was so burnt and desolated it was like walking through No Man's Land, especially because they'd been warned it was mined, so you never knew what Hank had planted, what death lay underground as well. Though I knew different, I said nothing. What would be the point? Knowing he'd bluffed them wouldn't gain Hank any posthumous pity from these men.

Floyd swills himself some Tonic and looks over at Al. "We seen worse," he says. "But you don't expect to find the Western Front right here in California. That Beecham was a devil, all right, to take his fifty thousand out of us. Twice now. Once with rain and once with fire. I'm glad that sonofabitch is dead. If he wasn't dead, I'd shoot him on sight. He deserved what happened to him."

"He chose what happened to him," I said.

"Yes, Doctor," snaps Al, "and he chose what happened to us too."

They went on in their terse way about the evidence, how the blaze must have been started from some point north of

the cauldrons. I could imagine the ribs of gunpowder laid
out, the fiery fan. And with a grim glance toward me, they
said that, yes, Hank Beecham had done what he'd promised:
he had died where he stood. And what little was left of him,
the sheriff took to the morgue, that and the sword.

CHAPTER ELEVEN

The sword troubled me. Nagged and prickled and poked at me all the way back to my office. The rifle was a thing worth having. But the sword? *You could slay a whole regiment with a sword and never have rain.* Gnawing on this bothersome thought, I take the mail out of the box, unlock my door, go into my study, take off my hat and put it on Blanche's head. I reach in the desk drawer and find my own bottle of Majic Bitters Tonic, uncork it, and put it to my lips. Put it down. Throwing the mail on the desk, I see my letter to Miss Emmons, returned to me unopened. On the back in a spidery copperplate hand was written, *My sister has left here. You cannot find her again. A.K.*

I could just imagine Miss Emmons receiving the letter, knowing full well what was in it. I could imagine her ordering the obedient Agnes to return it unopened, telling Agnes exactly what to write, so that nothing should be left undone, so her position should be absolutely clear and forever final.

The telephone jangles and I go to it. It's the county coroner. He asks me to come to the morgue and identify the remains. He says it's a formality. Someone has to sign the form, and it should be the next of kin, but lacking that, it should be a medical man. "You should be a medical man!" I yell into the box on the wall (no doubt the operator getting an earful too). "You should be a medical man. The coroner should be a doctor, not an elected sowbelly whose sole wish is to put your snout in the public trough and whose sole talent is licking your way up the voters' legs to their pockets!"

"Take it up with the voters next election, Doctor," says the coroner (who I think is one of Lew Cannon's sons-in-law, some relation like that). "I'm calling you because you're a doctor and you seem like next of kin to that madman. Come in and sign the form and we'll get these remains disposed of."

I felt suddenly damp handed, dry mouthed. "What do you mean, disposed of?"

"They ought to be buried, I suppose. Rightfully, but they're not, well, it's not as if it's a body. It's bones."

"You're goddamn right they ought to be buried!"

"Burials cost money. I don't even say funeral. Even a mere burial costs money, the grave, gravediggers. The city shouldn't have to pay. We're all agreed on that. Beecham nearly destroyed us."

"Who's all agreed?"

"We. The city. The city and county officials. The—"

"I know who." I hung up.

I went directly to the bank, to Art's office, told the girl at the typing machine I wanted to speak to him. (She wasn't a girl, actually. Art had dispensed with girls and hired a gorgon to protect him.) She took the message in and came back out and said he'd be a minute.

More like twenty minutes. But I sat, turning my hat in my hands, watching while work crews with pulleys and ladders struggled to get the bank's central chandelier back up into the high ceiling. Mercifully, no one had been beneath it when it fell in the blasts. When at last the gorgon said I could go into Art's private sanctum, I didn't even wait for her to close the door behind me. I walked straight to Art's desk and I said, "You owe it to Hank Beecham to bury what's left of him."

"I don't owe Hank Beecham duck dung."

"You owe it to him to bury his bones. You owe it to him to pay for a funeral."

"Why?" Art takes off his glasses, eyeballs me defiantly.

"Because you by God hired him in 1916! And you by God owed him fifty thousand dollars! And you by God owe it to him to bury what little is left!"

"Surely, there is some city agency empowered to bury the indigent." A little ferrety grin lit his face. "Though I don't see why we should bother with the charred remains of a madman, a lunatic."

"Death cures everything, Art."

"Beecham was a—"

Ping.

"—lunatic."

Ping.

"Let Miss Emmons bury his bones in—"

Ping.

"—Chagrin. He was her—"

Ping. Splash. Splatter.

"—husband."

We both looked out the window. Drops. Raindrops. Ping. Splash. Rattle went the window. Rumble went the distant thunder. I walked out of the office and into the bank, Art right behind me. Noise in the bank had hushed. Working-men on their ladders, tellers at their tills, clerks with their papers, customers, all of us silent save for our footsteps moving in unison toward the window and the door, which someone flung open. There came the damp breath of rain. Rain hitting the sidewalks, rain streaking dust-and-soot-caked windshields, cars polka-dotting with rain that now came down like lumps of hard candy. The ping turned to pelt. I moved outside with the rest of them. I stood beside Art Whickham in the rain. I said again, "You owe it to him to bury what's left."

CHAPTER TWELVE

S lap, slap, slap, doing its best against the driving rain, the wiper swept across the Ford's front window as I left the bank and drove straight to the county morgue. I told the young lady there to go tell that elected fool I was here.

She must have known who I meant, because the coroner came right out, wearing a suit and a smile, bristling with borrowed efficiency. I told him the city would pay to bury this much of Hank Beecham. "You send these remains to the undertaker and say they are to be buried in the city ceme-tery, in the same grave with Eulalie Beecham, the sword too. You send Art Whickham the bill."

"The final resting place is not my responsibility, Doctor," says the coroner. He is a slick, smooth-faced young man, pink, bland as rice pudding. "My job is to get you to sign these forms, and then the remains can be released to the next of kin. I guess that's you too."

"You put down the city of St. Elmo as the next of kin. You send the bill to Art Whickham. Finally, he's going to pay for something."

Whatever the coroner thought, he kept it to himself, and I followed him down a hall to a frigid room tiled in black and white. He turns on the electric light because the blinds are all decently drawn. Still, you could hear the rain noisily sluicing down and slopping in the gutters.

Just then, a young attendant (probably another of Lew's relatives) wheels in a cart, and on it are a pair of metal boxes, still smoking because they've just taken them off the ice. The sword is lying there beside them. It had been wiped clean of soot. It did not shine, but it was clean. The attendant goes over to one of the counters and picks up a tweezers, pliers, and some scissors, all just lying about, not sterile and not kept from dust or dirt. He uses the tweezers first to try to pull the pin out of a latch on one of the metal boxes, but it seems to be frozen shut, so he uses the pliers. I am disgusted, but silent. He gets the pins pulled at last and the lid comes off and the four sides fall open. There are the bones.

The bones were not clean as the sword. They were not varnished and mute like Blanche. These bones testified graphically to a more immediate and violent death. Dirt clung to them, bits of tissue, a small patch of scalp with singed hair on the portion of cranium. Two teeth bloodied in the mandible. They were all fragmented. A few knobby vertebrae, one with a rib still joined, an ulna, a portion of the pelvic structure, femur, none of it connected. The force had blown him apart. The coroner looked woozy. The attendant too. "Nothing more democratic than bones," I say. "The best of us, the worst, the kindest, the cruelest. All men's bones are created equal."

The coroner swallows, smiles, and nods sagely. He'll probably run for Congress next.

The attendant lifted the second box, smaller, laid it on the table. This box opened more easily. There was the hand, badly charred, the skin tattered and fragile, thin, flapping in tiny patches. I ask the attendant for a magnifying glass, more light, and a sterile probe and scalpel.

"Why sterile?" asks the coroner. "You think he's going to get sick?" The attendant laughs through his nose.

Paying them no mind, I probe the tissue (what little there is), turning it carefully, examining each of the metacarpals, which are not those of a man who cracked his knuckles for half a century. As for such flesh as remained, what wasn't burned was bloated and black. I went back to the bones, to the bit of mandible, a portion of the right half.

"He's dead, Doctor," the coroner declares. "What is there to study? We're busy here, and like you say, all men's bones are created equal." He thrust at me the form and pen. "Are you going to sign or not?"

I signed. Oh, I signed. And without another word to that fool or his apprentice fool, I got back in the Ford.

Rain billowing out behind my tires like full hoops of crinoline, I go through town, and everyone on the street, their hats are slouched down, their collars turned up. Those rainy faces are fearful, fearful as the days we fought the fire. We fought the fire and won, and now we are all wondering if we are going to have to fight the rain as well. Everyone wondering if it is going to be, *After Hank, the deluge.*

I leave the Ford chugging, idling at the sheriff's and dash in, shaking off my hat in the doorway. Some of the men are at the windows watching the rain, including Floyd and Al. "Listen, boys," I begin. "You didn't say, I mean, when you went out to Shiloh after the fire, you never mentioned a truck. Did you mention a truck? Did I miss it? Did you find a truck burnt? The remains of a Dodge truck?"

Floyd and Al regard each other like they are sifting through each other's memories. They ask where this truck would have been.

"Behind the shack."

"The shack was gone. Only the cookstove stood. That

and the shells of the cauldrons. Everything else was burnt to a stubble."

"But the hand, the sword, where were they?"

"All that was well beyond the shack. North of it."

"Could you find that place again, where the bones and sword were found? Could I find it?"

"What are you looking for?"

I could not say, and perhaps the boys just took pity on me, because finally one of them said that the remains of the cookstove would show where the shack had stood, and that there was no melted-down truck behind it, but that at each place where they had found human remains, I would find a red rag tied to a wooden stake driven into the ground. Where they'd found the sword, there was a blue rag tied to a stick. They did that always as a matter of policy, marked the place where they found evidence or bodies, because sometimes the information was needed in court.

"There is no court for this," says Floyd, looking out again at the rain mottling the window. "Beecham will be judged before heaven for this, and he will go to hell."

CHAPTER THIRTEEN

I drove north to Shiloh. I had to satisfy myself that the truck was not there. The boys would not have missed a melted-down truck, but they might not have looked for it either. They would not have known to look. And maybe the Dodge truck had got moved from behind the shack. Well, I would not miss it. However much of it had melted, and wherever the Dodge truck had last endured that fiery furnace, I would find it. If it was there, I would find it.

The Ford wouldn't go as fast as I needed to go. I must get there before something escapes me, some lost possibility, some message I might yet miss. The windshield wiper cannot keep up with the rain pouring, lashing the old Ford, and the window starts to steam up on the inside. I reach for a handkerchief to wipe the glass clean, but my hand closes on my letter to Martha Emmons. I pull it out, and despite the difficult road, the poor light, the rain that has smudged the envelope, I read again, *My sister has left here. You cannot find her again*, in Agnes Kreuger's aged copperplate hand.

She is a good girl. Reliable.

I guessed as much. Agnes did as she was bid. She was the widow of a military man, and used to taking orders. She wrote on the envelope and returned it to me. Agnes Kreuger had told me the truth. But it was not forever final. Only death is forever final. *Only death*, I told myself, hearing too Miss Emmons's voice, *Love alone love alone*, as I drove on and on through the ruination everywhere evident, the wreckage, the destruction wrought by fire and now by rain. The road out to Shiloh was a dirt road, wrecked and rutted, the earth scorched as by a retreating army burning everything in its path, everything the enemy might use. As far as the eye could see, the groves (Doradel mostly) were burnt to stumps, seared and silent sentinels, the sort of horror I remembered from pictures of No Man's Land during the Great War, all of it drenched and dripping, the desolation everywhere of such great miserableness that the Ford seemed to forge on through hell.

But I got to Shiloh. Floyd and Al had told truly. It had all been burnt to stubble, the stubble deluged with rain, muddied beyond recognition.

But yes, the cookstove stood, all blackened but miraculously upright where the shack had been. There was no burnt-out Dodge nearby, but I was determined to walk Shiloh till I found it, or satisfied myself it was not to be found. I pulled my hat down and my coat collar up, and in the merciless falling rain, I started toward the stove. I could see debris everywhere, shattered glass, and here and there fragments you could recognize, a cook pot maybe, a fry pan, even some skeletal remains of the fallen towers in the distance, and closer by, the shells of cauldrons lolling, rain striking them hard, like forlorn drumbeats. Well beyond the shack, I sighted the little stakes with their limp red flags, the blue one where they'd found the sword, and I went toward them. I trod this barren ground looking for—what? I no more knew why I had come here than Hank had known when he returned that night in 1916, when Horace and Earl had slathered themselves all over him, producing, finally, the pair of boots they swore belonged to Eulalie, expecting, hoping Hank would pay for them, for a piece of the past. But the boots were no more Eulalie's than that hand and mandible at the morgue were Hank's. Hank might have paid for the Enfield. But he would not have thought the sword worth having. Not then. Not ever. He was a man whose grace lay in his absolute mastery of what he did well, did without meaningless gesture or squandered effort, as an artist does something well, though Hank claimed he did not believe in art, only science.

He had put the grid of science over history, distilled instinct through precision, come up with something fluid, rehearsed, perfectible. *You could slay a whole regiment with a sword and never have rain.* The sword was not his. The hand was not his. Who died at Shiloh?

That's what I asked myself over and over as I walked the muddy field, from picket to sodden picket marking the places where remains had been found, the one flagged with blue quite a bit to the north. Rain soaked through my coat, and my trousers flapped wet around my legs. As I trod from stake to stake, every step I took over that dreadful ground was wrung from me. Mud flowed over my shoes, oozed, sucked at my feet as if trying to draw me down into its domain, refusing to release me for the next step toward the next flag. The afternoon light was slowly fading, and at each stake and flag, I first knelt and felt, then fell to my knees and crawled on all fours, my fingers splaying through the mud, clawing the mud, drawing up clumps of it, prodding, using my hands on it like the mud had a body and I, the doctor, would by God dig until I found out what ailed it. And finally, I did.

At the third stake, I found what I had come for. On my hands and knees—rain drenching through my clothes and my doctor's hands brown-bloodied with mud—I grabbed the wet earth till finally my fingers found what I had been looking for all the time without knowing that's what I was look-ing for. Buttons. I closed my fingers round them and slowly pulled my hand from the protesting mud, got to my feet and stood, palm out, so that the rain could wash the buttons clean. Brass buttons. Union insignia. Genuine Union, if not genuine Union general. They were charred up and so small it's no wonder the sheriff's boys missed them. You'd have to know they were there. As I had known they were. I turned them over one by one, regarded them, and thought to myself, it's true: *Only a fool would go into battle, buttons in one hand, epaulettes in the other.*

That was Earl Beecham's hand. That was Earl Beecham's sword. These were Earl Beecham's buttons. Earl was enough of a fool. Earl would have run into battle with buttons in one hand, sword in the other, foolishly swinging it overhead. I could see him. Earl was a fool, all right. What had he said? A racehorse and a race whore and going to Mexico for real whiskey, not a Tonic brewed by the sons of slaves. Earl Beecham would have never got to Mexico. Not with his thirst. He couldn't have gone that long without a drink. He would never have made it to the border, not with a thousand dollars burning in his pocket and that thirst on him. He probably got as far as the next county. Found himself some brothel, some speakeasy (maybe the latter first, to work himself up for the former). I could imagine Earl Beecham pissing drunk in a darkened speakeasy, buying the camaraderie of the men and the affection of the women, and working himself into the same pitiless rage as Jeremiah. It was as

Hank said: Earl, like Jeremiah, needed a war. And lacking that, he could be found creating one, collecting lots of listeners, people sure to stay close (especially as Earl was buying), people drunkenly enchanted with his glorious stories of Patrick Cleburne, the fightin'est Irishman ever, leading the doomed Yell Rifles through a thicket of bullets at Shiloh. The Union general, sword raised, about to lay waste to Jeremiah Beecham, then falling at Jeremiah's feet with a bullet through the brain, Jeremiah taking the sword from the slain commander's still-warm hand and cutting off his buttons and his epaulettes, getting on the general's horse, riding into history, legend, and the thick of that terrible day. Oh, it was probably just glorious the way Earl told it! And imagine his rancor and outrage when he came to the part about the pawnshop and the place of honor above the counter, the trophies that Jeremiah had so gallantly fought for vanishing before they could be redeemed. And probably there were men in Earl's audience who vowed they knew this story, men who knew of Shiloh, knew of Jeremiah's deeds, knew the very sword and buttons and epaulettes Earl spoke of, knew in fact where that very sword hung, where it could yet be redeemed. They would have staggered themselves down the street to the pawnshop, where the story got told all over again and Earl got assured: *These are the sword, the buttons, the epaulettes, genuine Union general. Redeem them, sir, and redeem your family's honor.* And that's probably just what Earl did. With his thousand dollars, he redeemed the family's honor, got back on the racehorse he'd bought, rode like hell back to the old family plantation.

I put the buttons in my pocket. Probably the epaulettes were around here too, not far from one of the other stakes, the red flags sodden now in the rain. I did not look for them. The buttons were enough for me. I slogged back in the direction of the Ford, the rain coming down in silvery sheets like mercury, making the way before me almost opaque, but as I came again to the cookstove where the shack had been (and no truck, melted or otherwise, anywhere that I saw) and looked at the shells of the three cauldrons, useless as spent artillery, I quit walking. I stood and let the rain wash over me. I wondered. Considered. *Wait. Think. Ask another question. Imagine.* Imagine Earl riding up here on his racehorse with his trophies. How would Hank have greeted him? The man I had last seen out here had his Enfield aimed at me, and fired, by God! He fired at me! Would Hank have welcomed the sound of hooves? Hank expected the army. Hank would have thought he was being attacked. Hank would have blown Earl right out of the saddle. Earl would have died. But not in fragments.

I mopped my hot face with wet hands. *Hank was not here.*

The cauldrons yet burned when Earl rode up, and the shack was still stacked with gunpowder and dynamite and arms. But Hank was not here. The phosphorous, sulphur, saltpeter, and whatever the hell else he used, the vials and weights and ladles, Hank would have smashed all that so his formulas could never be deduced by anyone. But Hank was not here. The wind alone greeted Earl Beecham as he staggered in, full of loot and liquor. I could see Earl drunkenly crashing into the darkened shack, wrecked chemicals, broken glass everywhere, Earl whooping the Rebel yell, swinging his sword, ready for the fighting and refighting of Shiloh, calling, *Uncle Hank, looky here! Looky here what I got, Hank!* I could see Earl spinning off the splintery porch, checking the privy maybe, lurching all over Shiloh, calling out for Hank and heedless of the embers that yet burned and twinkled beneath those chemical cook pots. Perhaps the incendiary fan was laid, or some portion of it. It would not have taken much, and Earl would not have noticed. The horse would have, though. The horse would have spooked and bolted, like Hank's animal had in 1917, its every instinct forewarning danger. But such few instincts as Earl had would have been dulled by drink and bloated by pride, and so he staggered through Shiloh, a foot soldier, an infantrymen like his grandfather, buttons in one hand, epaulettes in the other, stopping only to stab the sword into the ground while he fumbled for a cigarette. The hilt of the sword rocked slowly back and forth while Earl struck his match, lit his cigarette, flung the match behind him. Maybe he even smoked the cigarette, flipping the still-glowing butt toward the cauldron, perhaps toward the gunpowder ribs of the incendiary fan. Then, waving the sword overhead, Earl whooped his Rebel yell and ran northward, the Battle of Shiloh yet before him, the chance to fight it, to right it, to redeem it, all that glowing at him from a distance.

Hank Beecham did not even set the blaze that nearly took our town. That's how I finally pieced it together. He got in his Dodge truck and left the St. Elmo Valley to stew in its own smugness, perhaps, but he did not start the blaze that nearly consumed us. He had set it all in motion, though, and then he drove away. He put Shiloh behind him. Grant too. Cleburne. Even Jeremiah, whose valor and luck throughout the War had brought him only to drink and despair and cruelty endlessly inflicted on his wife and children. These were casualties of Shiloh: Horace and Earl, Virginia and Eulalie, the other two brothers, Jeremiah. They should all have been counted with the dead in 1862, though the Beecham children were not yet born. Hank alone survived Shiloh, survived the fire and the rain. The two forever united. But the battle was behind Hank now, and in leaving it, he'd put Eulalie behind him too. Perhaps there was no peace for Eulalie, but there might yet be for Hank. Maybe now Hank could ask for time's mercy, time's forgiveness. Maybe now time would mean something to him. It should. It must.

Like Hank, I put Shiloh behind me. In the last of the December afternoon, I drove away from that scarred and luckless scrap of land. But not in the same direction Hank had driven.

Hank had followed the road leading to Jesuit Pass, had gone over the pass and down the other side, east, into the white desert. *My sister has left here.* I'm sure she has, Agnes. I'm sure you're telling me the truth, Agnes, and your sister has gone where I will never find her again. I will never find either of them, but they will have found each other. I can imagine Hank standing at the faded house in Chagrin, tall, unstooped, erect as the surrounding date palms, and Agnes (knowing exactly who he was to look at him, to look at his hands, his deteriorating jaw) leading him to Martha, who waits in the parlor. I can see Miss Emmons, composed, chin lifted, no longer fretting her collar, the ghost of all those endearing young charms playing about her lips. And I know what she would have been thinking too: *Love alone.* They had both been through the refiner's fire, all the inessentials purged. And now anyway, love alone was essential.

As I near town, I notice that the rain no longer pocks, splatters, pelts the windows of the Ford. It's just rain now, not terrible rain. Just rain. I peer out the window. There is a long thin bronze streak visible in the west. A slit of sky, a shard of sunset. Maybe the rain will let up tomorrow. Maybe tomorrow the rain will even end and the funeral can be held in peace. Neither fire nor rain, but peace. Though I might be the sole mourner at that funeral tomorrow, I will go, resolved to throw these Union buttons in the grave with Eulalie, the sword, and what was left of Earl, the last of the Beechams. Say what they will at the funeral, farewell to Hank, I will not contradict them. I had struck a trust, an accord, a peace with Hank Beecham, and I will keep it. Hank did not want peace. He wanted victory. And maybe now he had it. He had kept his vows anyway, and they were forever final. He had never forgotten. *You'll never forget this, Doctor.* And I never would.